BENEATH THE NEON EGG

Fiction
The Copenhagen Quartet
Kerrigan in Copenhagen, A Love Story
Falling Sideways
In the Company of Angels

Getting Lucky: New and Selected Stories, 1982–2012
Last Night My Bed a Boat of Whiskey Going Down
A Passion in the Desert
Cast Upon the Day
The Book of Angels
Drive Dive Dance & Fight
A Weather of the Eye
Unreal City
Crossing Borders

Nonfiction
Riding the Dog: A Look Back at America
The Literary Traveler (with Walter Cummins)
Realism and Other Illusions: Essays on the Craft of Fiction
Winter Tales: Men Write about Aging (as editor, with Duff Brenna)
The Book of Worst Meals (as editor, with Walter Cummins)
Writers on the Job: Tales of the Non-Writing Life
(as editor, with Walter Cummins)
The Girl with Red Hair (as editor, with Walter Cummins)
Andre Dubus: A Study of the Short Fiction

BENEATH THE NEON EGG

A Novel

THOMAS E. KENNEDY

BLOOMSBURY

NEW YORK • LONDON • NEW DELHI • SYDNEY

Published by Bloomsbury USA, New York

Bloomsbury is a trademark of Bloomsbury Publishing Plc

All papers used by Bloomsbury USA are natural, recyclable products made
from wood grown in well-managed forests. The manufacturing processes
conform to the environmental regulations of the country of origin.

A 9,500-word novella entitled "Autumn Wasps," which ultimately grew into this novel,
appeared in 1999 in *Agni* and was nominated for a Pushcart Prize by Maxine Kumin,
former Poet Laureate of the United States and a winner of the Pulitzer Prize for poetry.

An excerpt appeared in altered form in *Epoch* magazine and in *Frank: A Journal of
Contemporary Writing & Art* in 2001, was nominated for a Pushcart Prize, and received
the Frank Expatriate Writing Award in 2002 at the Geneva Writers' Conference.

Material in this novel appeared in altered form in the 2003 book *Bluett's Blue Hours*.

The quote concerning hailstones is from Jonathan Raban's "The
Unlamented West," in the *New Yorker*, May 20, 1996.

The Latin palindrome in chapter 4 is copyright Lars Rasmussen and is used here with his kind
permission. The quotes from Kaj Munk and from Dan Turèll's "Charlie Parker on Isted Street"
are translated by Thomas E. Kennedy, the latter with the kind permission of Chili Turèll, and were
first published in *Poet Lore*, vol. 107, nos. 1–2, Spring-Summer 2012. With thanks to Barry Lereng
Wilmont for his facilitation of permission for the translation. And with thanks to Daniel Kennedy
for advice on how to represent Halfdan E's statement about Miles Davis's *Aura* in chapter 5.

The lines quoted in chapter 9 are from Shakespeare's "Sonnet 29," from William Blake's "The Sick
Rose," from John Keats's "A Thing of Beauty Is a Joy Forever," from John Milton's "Paradise Lost,"
from Michael Drayton's "Idea," and from Dan Turrèll's "I Should Have Been a Taxi Driver."

LIBRARY OF CONGRESS CATALOGING-IN-PUBLICATION DATA

Kennedy, Thomas E.
Beneath the neon egg: a novel / Thomas E. Kennedy.—First U.S. edition.
pages cm
ISBN 978-1-62040-141-5 (alk. paper)
1. Irish Americans—Fiction. 2. Divorced men—Fiction. 3. Male friendship—Fiction.
4. Aliens—Denmark—Copenhagen—Fiction. 5. Psychological fiction. I. Title.
PS3561.E4277B47 2014
813'.54—dc23
2013042336

First U.S. edition 2014

1 3 5 7 9 10 8 6 4 2

Typeset by Hewer Text UK Ltd, Edinburgh
Printed and bound in the U.S.A. by Thomson-Shore Inc., Dexter, Michigan

Bloomsbury books may be purchased for business or promotional use. For information on bulk
purchases please contact Macmillan Corporate and Premium Sales Department at specialmarkets@
macmillan.com.

For Daniel, Isabel, Søren, and Leo
And for the Mademoiselle

And with deep and sincere thanks to
Anton Mueller, Helen Garnons-Williams,
and all their colleagues at Bloomsbury
and to Nat Sobel, Judith Weber, Roger Derham,
Alain de Botton, Junot Díaz, Andre Dubus III,
Duff Brenna, Bob Stewart, Walter Cummins,
Greg Herriges, and Gladys Swan

Words, sounds, speech, men, memory, thoughts,
fears and emotions—time—all related . . .
all made from one . . . all made in one . . .
Thought waves—heat waves—all vibrations . . .
—John Coltrane, *A Love Supreme*

CONTENTS

I.   ACKNOWLEDGEMENT   1

1.   No, Woman, No Cry   3
2.   Aura—Intro   9
3.   It's So Easy to Fall in Love   21
4.   A Night in Tunisia   40
5.   Aura   51
6.   Noise Rock: Arab on Radar   61
7.   The Crystal Ship   73

II.   RESOLUTION   95

8.   Groovin' High—Aura Yellow   97
9.   The Damned Don't Cry   111
10.   Blood Count   116

III.   PURSUANCE   123

11.   Bad Religion   125
12.   Equinox   135
13.   Like Paradise   145

IV.   PSALM   157

14.   A Love Supreme   159

PART I

ACKNOWLEDGEMENT

That silence is loud.

—Miles Davis

1. No, Woman, No Cry

Friday Bluett follows desire, abandons his work, escapes to the wild.

He takes the train from Copenhagen Central Station to Hillerød, and catches the four o'clock north from there—"the Prairie Express," Benthe called it, and he can see why. There are only two train wagons, and they clatter across the flat, mid-January fields of north Zealand through the falling snow. His car is empty and cold. Bluett hunches in his leather coat, black wool Kangol pulled low on his forehead, long gray scarf knotted at his throat. This winter has been the coldest he's seen in twenty years of Denmark. Beneath his black jeans he wears flannel pajama pants, his feet shod in engineer boots over thick wool socks.

He stares out the window at the snow sketching down the already dark, late winter afternoon, and remembers his Discman, clicks it on and hears the formal opening phrases of Coltrane's *A Love Supreme*, which swell his heart with acknowledgement of his existence. *That I exist is acknowledgement*, he thinks. He feels good. Free. His ex hated jazz. Lately he has been trying to listen through all the way to the end of that symphony, but somewhere Trane loses him as he approaches the point where the music dissolves into pure vibration. When he gets there this time, he clicks it off, removes his earbuds.

He lifts the little *kylling* bottle of snaps from his coat pocket, screws the cap off and tips a third of it into his mouth, slips it back, with his knuckle wipes the under edge of his mustache.

Looking out at the countryside, foreign as it is, he realizes that he feels at home now. Earlier, too, when the train from Copenhagen traversed a long, gently winding street of yellow brick apartment buildings, darkened by automobile exhaust—which once had seemed so foreign to him, so unfriendly, especially in winter—he felt easy. Now he knows the place, knows where it is in relation to other parts of the city and the country, knows how to negotiate the geography by bus or train or on foot, even by bicycle. He left the car with his ex. He doesn't need a car. She has the house, too, and he is happy to be free of it. All he wants is his apartment.

He feels at home here now, despite the fact that he is divorced, faces the future alone. Not alone. With his kids. Who both live in Copenhagen and have started at the university. When he was married, he and his wife didn't do anything. They worked, visited her family for birthdays, Christmas, Easter, took vacations in the parents-in-law's summer house. The calendar of their years was irrevocably filled. They didn't go anywhere, *do* anything—but get on each other's nerves.

Now he is free to explore, to adventure. He is discovering his new city, his new country, and he likes it. Now he has a future. Not just more sameness. As he looks out at the snow blowing across the flat landscape, he realizes that once forty-three seemed old to him; now it just seems adult. He remembers once as a young father of thirty dancing with an "older" woman at a party who pressed against him, looked into his eyes—how old she seemed.

At the same time, he halfway wonders what he is doing; why is he taking a series of trains to go up into the northernmost reaches of Zealand to meet another man's wife in the hopes of—and he is quite certain this will happen—what is the term? Fucking her? Mutual seduction. The woman he is meeting is extremely attractive. They have been flirting for months, but he wonders if it is good to allow himself to be carried on the tide of his desire like this. With the secretary of one of his most important business contacts to boot.

He thinks about her face, her body, her eyes, her sexy mouth . . . Well, who could resist that? Why should he?

The conductor steps through the car, checks Bluett's ticket, and Bluett asks him in Danish to be let off at Halvstrand.

"You don't want Hundested?"

Bluett smiles secretly, tickled by the word. Hundested means literally Dog Place. "No, Halvstrand." Which means Half Beach. Everything means something in this country.

"That's a summer house area," the conductor says. "Nothing there." He has a series of tiny yellow warts that wiggle on his cheek as he speaks.

"*Jeg skal mødes med nogen,*" Bluett says. I'm being met.

The conductor shrugs his shoulders and his mouth, warts bobbing, and moves off, but looks back again. "You speak good Danish. You American? Wouldn't know it," and he moves off to the other car. Bluett takes the *kylling* from his pocket again and burns his tongue agreeably. He has another, larger, half-fifth bottle in the other pocket of his coat along with another CD of *A Love Supreme*. House gifts for Benthe. And three joints purchased on Pusher Street in the Free State if she's of a mind to smoke them with him. He drinks off the rest of the *kylling* bottle to still his nerves, remembering how her blue eyes met his as she said, "Henrik won't be arriving until late Saturday afternoon. So why don't *you* come Friday evening? I will meet you at the train if you call me from Hillerød." Her gaze lingered on his.

He guesses she's not quite ten years older than him, fifty, fifty-two maybe, and he remembers that "older" woman dancing at the party—she was even younger than Benthe. But Benthe looks sexy as hell, the secretary of his contact at the pharmaceutical firm that gives him much of his translation work. To his eye she looks just like Julie Christie looked in *Doctor Zhivago*. The first time he went to her office, she was wearing tight beige leather jeans, her bottle-blonde hair plaited into one long braid that hung like a plumb line down to her rump. She greeted him with a handshake but held his hand in her soft fingers and asked, "Should we call you Mr. Bluett or Bluett or Patrick?"

"Why don't you just call me Blue—everybody does," he said, thinking *You can call me anything you want*—which she must have read in his gaze because her smile stayed on him, her eyes moving to his mouth. "Your mustache is red as copper," she said.

At that first meeting she gave him a company pocket Dictaphone. "For when we have rush work," she explained. "You can just dictate, and I shall type it for you."

As their ease with one another progressed and they spoke more casually, began slowly to flirt, he told her he read a lot, which seemed to impress her. Onto one of the little Dictaphone tapes, he recorded "The Love Song of J. Alfred Prufrock" and told her, "I read a poem on this one. By T. S. Eliot." She phoned him next day to tell him how beautiful she thought it was. "You read so well. I listened to it over and over. Even in bed. My husband almost became jealous."

Not having considered she might be married (she didn't act it), he blurted, "Oh! I'm sorry!"

"Do not be," she said. "I like it. And I said *almost*."

The little train slows and the conductor leans in, calling, "Halvstrand next!" Bluett wedges the empty *kylling* between the seat and the window and rises, lists across the rocking car. As the train pulls into the station, he watches his indistinct reflection in the window of the door. He should have trimmed his mustache. The gray hairs. It is still snowing, and she stands waiting on the uncovered platform in a long sealskin coat and fur hat.

"Do you mind walking?" she asks.

"Shouldn't we take a taxi?"

Her laughter is musical. "There are no taxis here. And Henrik has our car in Copenhagen. I took the train up this morning. It's only fifteen minutes of walking. I shall keep you warm," she says and takes his arm, leaning into him with the whole side of her body, and he thinks it's really going to happen, finally. He manages not to think of her husband. Clearly she's not thinking of him.

The cottage is tiny on a broad, low property that extends to a tall, fenced-off cliff over the beach. Before they go in, she leads him against a heavy, whistling wind to the fence and they look down from the cliff to the sliver of strand, perhaps a hundred feet below. Moonlight filters through the falling snow and dark blue clouds, and he can see ice glinting on the sea, sand glittering silver beneath a layer of snow.

"God," he whispers. "It's so beautiful."

She huddles against him, against the wind. Her face is very close. She looks at his mouth, and he kisses her.

"This is better, isn't it?" she asks, and as he pulls her close to his body, she says, "Shall we not go in?"

They step through the deepening snow toward the door of the cottage.

"We are able to rent this because the owner cannot sell it; no one will buy it," she tells him. "The property gets centimeters smaller every year. In ten years the cliff will be almost up to the cottage." She shrugs, dismissing it. "I can taste you have been drinking snaps. I can taste it on your tongue." Her smile is flirty.

"The train was so cold."

"Well, we have things to warm you here," she says. "I forgot to tell you

6

Henrik's sister Dorte is here." Still with that smile, she adds, "She might want to warm you, too."

Inside, they stamp the snow off their boots. The cottage room is very small. There is a wood fire in a black metal stove beside an alcove with a broad bed spread with a brick-red cover, a large faded red oil painting on the one wall, small white-framed windows, a broad red kilim, whose color has been walked pale. A woman rises from an overstuffed white sofa. *Must be Dorte.* She is tall and thin and extends her hand. Her fingers are knotted, the knuckles swollen. But she looks no older than Benthe, who leans to Bluett's ear and whispers, "Dorte has not had a man in over a year."

Dorte slaps Benthe's arm. "Stop that!" she says, laughing, her face long and angular.

Next day, he catches the early afternoon Prairie Express back to Hillerød for the city train to Copenhagen. He wants to get out of there before Henrik shows up. He wonders whether he feels guilty or just uneasy about facing a man whose wife and sister he spent the night with.

It occurs to him, as the train bumps across the snowy flat countryside, how fleeting time is, how he had yearned for last evening and now it is behind him and he is being taken away from it. It turned into something other than he expected, and he doesn't know whether he liked it. He thinks he is probably finished with it and realizes how sorry he is about that, realizes that he feels more emotion for Benthe than he thought, but . . . Benthe would have been enough, but this was too much. A couple of times he was unfaithful to his ex, as he knows she had been to him, but it had not been so . . . Deliberate? Dedicated? It was too much. An image rises in his mind of the color of the faded red oil painting, the kilim, and sadness descends on him as he looks out over the white fields.

Then he warms to the thought he will be home in time to listen to some jazz CDs, drink some Stoli on the rocks. Maybe Sam is home, he thinks. Now he catches himself thinking about telling his friend and neighbor Sam Finglas all about it, is yearning to. As a war story. Which makes him wonder about himself. Is this stuff just something to tell about? Is that all it is? He cannot deny that the thought of telling Sam cheers him—but why should he need cheering up?

Smiling dreamily out over the rolling frozen countryside, he is excited by the memory of it, maybe more so than by the actual experience, the way Benthe, after three bottles of wine and much flirtation, got the three of them dancing, the way she took off her blouse, got them each to take off one piece of clothing at a time and when they were all down to their underpants, the way she herded them into the big bed in the alcove by the iron stove.

Something he'd always wanted, but he has to admit was not quite what he imagined. Benthe seemed somehow less desirable afterward, less attractive. Strangely less passionate. Scheming. Maybe that's why he fled before Henrik arrived. And he forgot to give her the Coltrane CD. They danced to Bob Marley and the Wailers. *No woman, no cry . . . What is that lyric all about anyway?*

He will be home early enough to get a full day's work in on Sunday, for the Friday he missed. To keep afloat, he has to do five pages of translation a day, five days a week. It is a good life, better than he ever expected. Far better than his aborted bank "career." Denmark needs a voice in what they call "the big world," and English is the lingua franca of the big world—"American," as the Danes say. At first he thought his language was being slighted, but they seem to prefer American, at least the new generations. The sun has set over the Empire. The U.S. is where the money is now. As long as it lasts. And Denmark. As good as the Danes are at English, they want their texts copyedited or translated from scratch to be certain they don't look foolish in the world. And there seems an unlimited amount of translation. And he doesn't have to worry about health care or university tuition for his kids. They even get a salary from the state for studying. All paid by taxes.

Americans are so afraid of taxes, he thinks, *of social democracy. Socialism is a scare word.* Yet he knows that if he was in the U.S. now he would be terrified of the future, afraid of being fired at a day's notice, losing a health care plan, the ability to send his kids to college. Here is civilization. Here is home now.

But there is something else about his life that he can't put a finger on.

Looking out over the white lowlands, he is aware of his thoughts, his emotions, but he is also aware that he does not know what he needs. He only knows that he has a need.

Then it occurs to him what the Bob Marley song is saying. There's a comma after the "no"—*no, woman, no cry . . .* It's a love song.

2. Aura—Intro

Bluett steps out of the dark, cold, empty Friday night, down the three steps to the semibasement west-side bar. He recognizes the music from the CD player behind the bar: Miles Davis and John McLaughlin doing Palle Mikkelborg's *Aura*. He knows the music of the Intro—spooky guitar notes, a background of horn, suddenly breaking loose into energy, blaring horn notes, icy guitar lines, tom-toms.

Standing in the doorway, he polishes the cold frost from his eyeglasses, puts them back on to survey the room. It seems an unlikely place for this music. The driving beat, the horn, searching, surveying, blaring, a few frantic guitar notes, bass, cymbals, piano, the searching, surveying trumpet again.

He has been out exploring, finding some interesting places, but this joint—a west-side Copenhagen dive, off Isted Street—he does not like the feel of, the look of the other men seated at tables drinking Black Gold and snow beer, a few with cheap-looking women, hard-faced. He should have gone straight home from the last joint, acknowledged the pointlessness of the night. What does he hope to find now? It is too late. He has wandered too far west in the city. Yet now he is here and the bartender looks his way.

"Double Stoli on the rocks, no fruit."

"Double *what?*" No flicker of humor lights this craggy Danish face.

"Stolichnaya. Vodka."

The bartender pours a double Absolut over an ice cube, chucks in a slice of lemon with his fingers and sets it before Bluett, takes his money. The trumpet is still searching against the background of percussion as he checks his watch—nearly two A.M.—and notices someone standing very near beside him. *Should have gone home.* He glances quickly. A tall, close-built, sandy-haired young man is standing much too near, staring at him. *Fuck. Should have gone home.* Bluett ignores him. Stares at the CD player, listens to the horn blaring, scaling, studies the glistening row of bottles, and the man leans closer.

9

Go away, please.

"May I be a little fresh," the man says in Danish, "and see what you have here," his fingers dipping toward Bluett's shirt pocket where he put his change.

Bluett's palm smacks the pocket flat to his chest. "No you may not!" he answers in Danish and looks away again, poised.

The man is still there. "You are not Copenhagener," he says. "From Jutland? Funen? Bornholm? Faroe Islands?" His words sweep across Bluett's face on a sour yeasty cloud.

Bluett swallows some vodka and says nothing, tensing his stomach muscles, poised for a fight, wondering if he will manage to get away with his teeth and skull intact.

But the younger man wanders away, over to one of the tables where a short, stout, dark-haired man sits, his face a thick-featured mask of stolidity, and Bluett watches surreptitiously, wondering what is in the idiot's mind as he performs the same number.

"May I be a little fresh?"

The trap of the seated man's rage unsprings instantly. He is on his feet, swinging, catches the sandy-haired man full in the mouth so blood creases his teeth as he staggers back from the blow.

I might not be old, he thinks, *but I am too old for this.*

The smaller man hits the sandy-haired guy again, and he topples backward over a table.

No one moves. They only watch. Bluett sees the face of a girl with thick makeup, hard smile, eyes bright.

Good night.

He drains the rest of the vodka, lifts his jacket from the hook beneath the bar and is up the three steps to the front door, out on the street in icy air, looking right and left toward Istedgade, anxious not to go the wrong way. He shuffles past a corner welfare shelter with men and women huddled in and outside the doorway, smoking, glowering at him, or lost in their own internal gloom. He glances at a man whose hand holding a cigarette to his mouth is dirty as the sidewalk. He passes a closed shawarma grill.

Not accustomed to this, out of practice. It is long since he has been out at this hour. What is he looking for? A woman? He thinks with regret of

Benthe. She turned out not to be at all what he expected, what he hoped for—but after all, she is married, and her husband and she are swingers, apparently. He had called to ask her out, but she had made a counter-proposal. She had invited him to a party, the kind of party where the host had a sauna and after dinner, she told him, all the guests get in the sauna and then they come out and dance to Greek music.

"It is exciting," she had said on the phone.

"What, uh, do they all take their clothes off?"

"Of course."

"I think I would be shy."

"You were not so shy two weeks ago in our country house."

"That was . . . spontaneous. And I was a little drunk."

"You could get a little drunk again. It is very exciting. All those naked bodies."

He thought of the naked men, many naked women, wondered where her head was. "Well, I think I'd just like to just see you. Besides, I'm not so much of a dancer."

It is tricky. She is the contact for his best customer. He has to extricate himself before it gets more involved. "Besides, I have a girlfriend now," he lied.

"You can bring her, too."

"I don't think she would like that."

"Well, if you change your mind. I still think you are a sexy." She says the last phrase in English.

Now he wonders what he is looking for. Just to see what's happening? The world has changed in the twenty years since he was alone.

He has only a vague sense of this area. To the right he knows is Halmtorvet, hookers, druggies. Bad news. He can see the Central Station looming up above the snaggle of buildings before him, aims for it. He can catch the S-train to Nørreport, Northgate, walk home from there.

The cold sidewalks are empty, dark, the black leather and pink and lavender dildos in porn shop windows dimly illuminated. An inflatable plastic woman sits in one window, her mouth a large O, her thighs spread around a plastic vulva. *Skamlæber*, they are called in Danish.

Shame lips. Same root as the English, Latin, *pudenda—pudere*, to be ashamed.

He looks up to a street sign, Viktoriagade, remembers a Dan Turèll poem about Charlie Parker playing a blue plastic saxophone on Victoria Street. Doubling back to avoid a group of beefy flaneurs, he passes a doorway from the shadows of which a woman asks, "You vant to come up with me?"

Bluett has not really considered this sort of alternative to loneliness. He pauses to look at her, feels himself swaying slightly, doubts that he would be able to muster passion for this woman, whose bare legs in a mini skirt are bone-thin and blue with chill. He looks at her face, which vaguely resembles the face on the statue in the harbor of the Little Mermaid, her dirty blonde hair short and choppy and her complexion, even shadowed, not the best. Could as well do it with an inflatable plastic doll. He is lonely, but not lonely enough to go with this poor creature in the shadows of that doorway, and neither does he wish to purchase company, at least not with money. But his heart goes out to her. Perhaps he would increase the sum of human misery by blatantly rejecting her. He gets a crazy idea then—a drunken idea that he acts on.

"How much just for a hug?" he asks.

Her face is impassive. "You can't buy no love affair, dude," she says. "You want French? Four hundred. Swedish? Three. Danish cost you five plus the room."

He knows what French is; Swedish, he guesses is a honeymoon of the hand; while Danish, he presumes, is the style of the missionary. He shakes his head, digs into his pocket for the fifty-crown note buried there, reaches it toward her hand which automatically rises to accept it, and he turns to move on, but she darts out from the shadows, brushes her lips against his cheek. Her blue eyes almost smile. He nods and continues walking, feeling a little better, but shuddering with the cold and the thought of the woman—the girl—in the shadowy doorway. He wonders if he is really far out enough to stop on a dark street to consider a poor, wretched hooker.

Shaking his head, he continues toward the Central Station, but somehow takes a wrong turn. Down an empty side street, a tall, thick-shouldered man steps out of a doorway in front of him and says in English, "You Dane? I am from Estland."

"Good for you," says Bluett and steps around him. The man circles back, slaps ten fingers to his own chest, says, "My body: five hundred crowns."

Bluett's heart lurches. "No," he says, zigzags past, but the man gets in front of him again. His face is high above Bluett's, his nose thick, his jaw, his neck.

"Okay okay, listen," he says. "My body: three hundred crowns!"

"What? Get lost. I'm not interested."

"You don't like me? Last offer: My body, one hundred crowns. Now and here!"

Bluett crosses the street, turning back precisely where he does not wish to go, deeper into the west side, sees a neon martini glass that he heads for just in case he will need to duck for shelter, but someone else is on the street behind him, and the Estonian lurches away toward the newcomer.

"You, yes," he says, "my Danish cousin. My body for you: four hundred crowns. Wery cheap bargain."

Bluett reaches the corner, sees the Central Station, mounts the stone stairway from the street to the elevated parking area, recognizing all at once the place where he finds himself now, a place he left behind when he was a kid, where hunger drives you out roaming, lonely sleepless nights. But he's not a kid now; he's forty-three years old.

I forgot about loneliness, but now I remember it again, I feel as lost as I ever have in my life even as I plan to tell my friend Sam about Benthe and Dorte, about the Estonian, the bar fight, the girl in the doorway, tell it light, good for laughs, when me and Sam swap war tales.

At the rim of the parking area, by the station front, several lone figures huddle in the icy dark. He recognizes the drunken unsteady movement of his feet toward the revolving door, considers how bad he would feel if one of his kids happened to be in there, see their father out alone at this hour, wandering, lost.

How can I explain it, kids? I am a man still. I am alone and I have not quite found my way yet. Play it cool. Invite them in for a beer. Talk. Yet it would break my heart for them to see that this life is not the life I raised them to. There was supposed to be a family unit here. There was supposed to be stability behind them, to nurture them through these university years. What would they make of all this? What would they think of their old man out on the town looking in all the wrong places for company, for solace, for someone to fucking talk to?

Regression, he tells himself. *That's what it is. Like when you were twenty-one years old, ending at three in the morning in Bickford's in New York staring dourly into a plate of scrambled eggs, a cup of weak coffee. Those years when you were a young banker. Now it's more than twenty years and a country later. Scandinavia. Standinavia. Copenhagen. Jazz city.*

You're lost, man.

The train pulls into Nørreport, and he climbs the stairs, thinks he will take a cab the rest of the way if there is one in the queue, but there is not. Only an empty, dark, cold street, which he crosses, past the geological museum, the national art museum, the botanical gardens, dark and withered in this freezing January night.

Then he is up to Sølvtorv, Silver Square, crosses it to Sølvgade, Silver Street, dark and empty at this time of night, and follows down to the frozen lake, stands for a moment on the corner looking across at the red neon Jyske Bank sign and the neon chicken laying neon eggs that glimmer in the black ice.

The outer door of his apartment building doesn't lock, but he has stopped worrying about that. Up the winding wood stairs, he pauses to look across at Sam's door, considers pounding on it. *Wake the bastard up. Tell him the story of your night.* He seriously considers it, looks at his watch. Almost three. He lays his ear against the scarred wood of the door and hears what sounds like the faint silken line of Getz's tenor. He taps lightly, and the music shuts down. He thinks he can hear someone listening on the other side of the door, taps again with a fingernail. "Sam!" he whisper-shouts hoarsely, clears his throat. "It's me. Blue."

The door swings open, and Sam's vivid, startled blue eyes peer out.

"Want company?" Bluett whispers, then repeats, in a normal voice, "Want company? I'm oiled but coherent. I think."

Sam turns the music up again—Getz blowing Brazilian stuff, Jobim, dreamy, very dreamy—and cracks a bottle of Danish stout and another of green Tuborg, pours from the two at once into the same glass—one for Bluett, one for himself. Black and tans.

"My dad used to mix the black stuff with champagne," says Bluett. "Drink it with raw oysters."

"Black velvet," Sam says. "Give you one hell of a hangover."

This apartment is the mirror image of Bluett's own. Instead of having its main view out onto the lake, it looks out over roofs and backyards, black angles silhouetted against the cold sky with its blurry, ghostly wafer of moon. Just one small window over the lake. The apartment is a mess of books, papers, sloppy stacks of things, dirty plates, hardened remains of coffee.

"Geez, you're a slob, Sam."

"There is order in my slop. As it is, I can find anything. Impose some artificial order on it and I wouldn't be able to find thing one."

Parched, Bluett empties half the glass onto his dry tongue, sighs, listens slit-eyed to Getz wailing elegance. Then he remembers the Estonian who stopped him earlier and tells the story, leaving out the fact that he was scared, telling it for a laugh. "You my Danish friend. Last offer: my body, fifty crowns!"

Sam's laughter is hearty, although Bluett sometimes wonders how genuine it is. Sam is his best buddy in the world, also divorced, also with grown kids, but Bluett sometimes feels he's never got beneath his friend's surface to where Sam really lives. *Or maybe it's just me. Maybe I'm the one who's all surface and cheap laughter.* He thinks about telling the story of Benthe and Dorte, but the desire to do so makes him feel cheap; instead he says, "So whas happenin', dude?"

Sam's lips go owlish in his delicate-featured black-Irish face.

"What's that look supposed to mean?" Bluett asks.

"*Look?*"

"That look on your Irish kisser. I know a look when I see it, and you got a look on. Written all over your . . ."

The smile spreads. "Met someone, you know? Of the female persuasion."

"You met someone of the female persuasion? Well, come on. Tell Uncle Pat. She got a sister?"

Sam's eyes go distant for an instant, and whatever they are seeing in that distance translates into purse-lipped pleasure.

The pleased lips tighten. He sighs. "I don't want to jinx it, Blue. It's too . . . tentative."

"Well, does she got a friend or not for crissakes?"

"All in good time, Blue. All in the fullness of time."

Across the hall again, with difficulty, he works his key into the lock of his door, lets himself in and realizes he is still wearing his coat, hadn't even taken it off at Sam's. He pees in the little water closet. Then is standing in the living room, staring out the windows to the frozen lake, thinks about Sam, the lucky dog. *You got to meet someone, too, fall in love.* He thinks of Benthe, Dorte, but doesn't want to go there—Benthe is married, and her arthritic sister-in-law wants some, too, and it's too much. Dancing to "Zorba the Greek" with a bunch of naked people! He thinks about another drink, a nightcap, some music on the CD player, a little night food: dark rye with salami and raw onion rings maybe, use the scissors to make confetti out of those chives on the kitchen windowsill . . . But suddenly the mere thought that he could make food, the mere thought that he has food and hunger, that he has shelter from the cold, the mere thought that he exists is acknowledgement, and it is enough.

Pitching his coat on the sofa arm, he moves to the bedroom, drops his pants on the hardwood floor, and is grateful to realize that by the time—by the fullness of time—his head touches the pillow he will be asleep.

He wakes in the dark, the incidents of the night slowly reassembling themselves in his consciousness, the pointless incidents. He reaches for his watch, presses the illumination button. Just past eight. Then he remembers it is Saturday and sighs with relief. He doesn't feel bad. Still drunk maybe, but in a good way. Horny way. In the dark, alone, meat in hand, he can go anywhere, do anything. Benthe is there with him then. And Dorte. The heat of their flesh, wetness of their mouths, their cunts, yes, the heat and hardness of his prick, yes, he will go to the sauna, dance naked, go down on Benthe in front of them all, she wanted me to lick my own come off her thigh—I wouldn't now—I would while her eyes blaze her lips full of lust, teeth glinting . . .

As his breath stills and his eyelids sag, he can feel the dreamy smile in the dark. Would be nicer to have a warm body beside him now, to stroke with his palm, his fingers. Tender. He wonders why he will do it in his mind alone but not with Benthe and the others. Maybe because the others would still be there afterward, when his passion was spent and it was all revealed as fantasy but with real people still there. He doesn't quite understand that. But remembers how it was to have Dorte there afterward up in Halvstrand. Couldn't get away fast enough.

And what you would do in heat and would repulse you after the fact. He thinks about a copy of *Playboy* he saved from a few years earlier, special on the thirtieth anniversary of the death of Marilyn Monroe. In it was a secret diary or transcript of a tape where she free-associated for her psychiatrist, and in which she claimed to have shaved Joan Crawford's pussy and gone down on her. Also claimed that her agent had her piss in a champagne glass and drank it. He wonders if it was true. Exciting to think of when you're hot, but repulsive when you're not.

Difference between fantasy and reality maybe. Or maybe because of my Catholic upbringing. Or maybe something else. Maybe I really don't like sex but need it, like the idea of it. Who knows? Maybe it's better than nothing. Maybe it has to be more than passion?

With his ex, their passion was so hot but burned out fast and then they had two children. Mistake to marry so young in heat. But if they hadn't, the kids would not exist. Is it so bad not to exist? Well, he wouldn't know, would he? Because there would be no one to know. Strange thought. Having no consciousness. No existence.

Do I like existing? Would I prefer not to?

Cannot deny I am as confused as when I was a teenager. More confused. Because then I believed in romantic love. Now I wonder whether it is all just to procreate and nothing more, to keep the species going and for what end? And we are useless as autumn wasps, men, after we have procreated, as Sam once put it.

He wonders whether the problem with Benthe is because she's married. That religious thing again. *The couple of times I fucked another man's wife— even while one of the husbands was passed out drunk in the next room. I performed without hesitation, not feeling I did anything at all wrong until afterward; the regret rushed in like a foul wave of sewer vapor. Learned this about myself and tended to avoid repeating that kind of behavior. But somehow the flirting with Benthe went too far for me to stop myself. Then she sprang Dorte on me with her arthritic fingers taking my stiff rod. Actually wasn't so bad. In memory. Kind of sweet. How she took it in her hand, fingers slow and careful in their deformity, and then looked into my eyes and smiled.*

Till afterward.

Once, before I married, even with the husband's consent. No, he directly asked me to because he wanted her to stop fucking some guy he hated. I knew about myself that I suffered moral hangovers that far outweighed the pleasure I got from certain things and that was one of those things. The five-year-old son of the father who gave me permission, asked me to, rattled the locked bedroom doorknob while I was fucking his mother and called through the door, "What are you doing in there, Mommy? What are you doing with Patrick?"

That was in 1972. I was eighteen. Just after my father died. The seventies was the wildest decade, wilder than the sixties. Now we've been through the eighties and more than half the nineties. And glad I am free of my ex, glad my children exist. But what's next?

Not more of the seventies. Not Benthe on their disappearing cliff with her arthritic sister-in-law or her nude Greek post-sauna dances with hopping cocks and jiggling breasts. Don't want to be with naked men.

The couple downstairs is having one of their very rare arguments, but it's a bad one, a divorce argument. Bluett can only hear the words of the wife, whose name he doesn't even know (*good fences make good neighbors*). In the course of what he hears, however, he learns the name of the husband when she says to him, "Know what, Jørgen? Know what? No one likes you. No one. Likes. You." Jørgen mumbles something, and she yells, "I don't fucking care if the neighbors hear! They don't like you either!"

Bluett holds his tongue, but is tempted to shout toward the floor, "*I* like him! But I don't like *you!*"

Soon he hears footsteps, the front door opening, closing. Then silence.

And inevitably Bluett is thinking of all the arguments he and his ex had. But at first it wasn't that way. When they met by chance in Copenhagen, Bluett on vacation with the money his father had left him, the fire between them was instant. And there was nothing to keep him in New York. He didn't much like his family—only his oldest sister—and he had an immediate facility for Danish that he never had for French or Spanish. And college was *free* here.

Problem was they married too young, didn't experiment enough, still had that in them, both of them, the urge for others, and contempt seeped in when the passion burned out for one another.

And what kind of life did they have? Bluett has to admit he was attracted to her family's affluence, father helped them buy a house in Brønshøj, on a hill over the expanse of boggy moor. That had its price, too—beholden to the affluent father-in-law. And the sense of adventure with which he came to Denmark, his love of jazz, soon was lost to the family requirements. And his ex, it turned out, *hated* jazz.

Their calendar was structured on family birthdays—brothers- and sisters-in-law, his ex's parents and aunts and uncles and cousins—the Danish holidays, the three days of Christmas, five days of Easter, a four-day Pentecost weekend . . . Not that they were religious; they observed all these "religious" feasts with food and drink. And they spent their vacations at their in-laws' summer house on the fjord.

Bluett didn't know his new country, he only knew his new family and their neighborhoods and the roads that led to them. And they didn't have any friends because their calendar was already filled. No time for new friends. And Bluett didn't much like going to jazz alone.

All the result of a very small inheritance from his father. Enough to take a vacation in Copenhagen, which he had always wanted to visit for its jazz. So he flew in on Pan Am, rented a room at the Imperial Hotel, alongside Vesterport Station, went to the old Montmartre jazz club and then the new Montmartre, saw Stan Getz and Gerry Mulligan there—switching horns, Getz playing baritone and Mulligan blowing tenor, and then heard Long Dexter on his tenor, too, and this was heaven, and he fell in love with the city. And then he fell in love *in* the city: One morning he asked a girl on Strøget, the Walking Street, for a match. He smoked then, and they didn't give free matches with the cigarette packs and he always forgot to ask to buy a box of stick matches, so he stopped a girl to ask for a light. It wasn't even a line.

But it led that day to their fucking four times in her west-side room, and to more passion and to romance, it led to marriage, to immigration, to children. And then the passion burned out, and what the heat concealed was all the things about each other that they could not bear and, in time, in twenty years, it led to divorce.

Lurid light is seeping in the windows over the frozen lake, and Bluett feels grief and regret and guilt seeping into his blood, and he can choose to stuff his face beneath the pillow, but he judges by the light that it is nearing ten, and his stomach growls.

He thinks of the brunch at O's, down the street, thinks of their eggs and bacon and beans and home fries and a big glass of tomato juice—maybe a bloody Mary—pictures himself munching happily while he leafs through the Saturday morning tabloid with its tales of violence and injustice and sex and photos of scantily clad women . . .

Saved by appetite.

3. It's So Easy to Fall in Love

What is time? he wonders. A work week is never so long. Neither is a weekend. A bottle of vodka is not so deep, a drink is shallow. But as he steps out of the shower, towels himself dry with Getz's "Sweet Rain" on the CD player, douses his jowls with the agreeable sting of his Armani aftershave, garbs himself in clean Calvin Klein briefs, Boss wife-beater, pin-striped Marimekko, binds a half Windsor in his old silk favorite, steps into fresh-pressed black jeans, bit worn about the cuffs, pulls on a sweater the color of the wine-dark sea and his trusty old lambskin, black Kangol backward on his pate, the world is so new again and full of hope.

It always starts again with hope.

Friday, blessed Friday. Time to open the gates of the world hidden behind the veil of matter. With the purest of elixirs. The sacrament of vodka. An allergist revealed this secret to him once when he was suffering from a bout of rhinitis. *If you must drink, drink vodka. The purest of drinks.* Her face rapt as she told him, her elephantine face like Lord Ganesha, remover of obstacles. *There have been cases of patients with acute, near fatal asthma attacks cured by vodka, one woman who had to drink two wine glasses of chilled vodka every hour to keep her lungs functioning under a drastic attack. Think about it.*

Bluett thinks about it as he lets himself out the door, wondering what Sam is planning for the evening. *I met someone.*

He descends the wooden staircase from his apartment and enters the freezing gloam of afternoon. A thief's start on *l'heure bleue*: red sun still hangs on the smoky horizon of the frozen lake. He waits a few respectful moments, watching his breath, watching the red glare from the far edge of Saint George's Lake, the old leper colony, as it stains the ice of Black Dam Lake.

In medieval times, Copenhagen stopped here, where he stands. No one was allowed to live beyond the lakes, only the lepers or a few tinkers whose shacks were razed during threat of invasion. Now, with Copenhagen no longer a gated city, this is part of the city center, this side of the lakes, and a million people live on the other side, the leper colony has been shut down, and Saint George, their patron, has joined the long line of dead saints. Bluett thrashes about in his mind for the source of that line—*my dead saints*—but cannot find it.

A dark-skinned, gray-eyed man, huddled against the cold, sidles past him, limping slightly, nods without meeting his gaze and enters the building next door to his own. A neighbor Bluett has never spoken to. Foreigner. South American, perhaps. Who? So many strangers so close to home.

The red ball of light sinks into the ice. Bluett waits for a taxi to pass, then crosses the blue road beneath the bare chestnut trees and steps out onto the ice. A lone skater makes lazy loops out in the center, gliding through the steepening dark, and Bluett trudges across the ice, his heart, his mouth, his brain yearning for the sacrament of vodka, his first drink of the week, of the weekend. He experiences this moment as worthy of a frieze on a Grecian urn. Drunk Stolis are sweet, those undrunk are sweeter yet.

To his right, across Fredensbro, the Peace Bridge, stands the tall white graffitied monolith of Fredensport, the Peace Gate, slanting up phosphorescent into the dusk, a keyhole cut into the middle of its flank. A door that will not open, falling but never completing its fall.

Pranksters once climbed it in the dead of night and shoved an enormous skeleton key into the carved keyhole at its center, some two stories above the grass. Bluett was offended. He has come to treasure that everfalling monolith. It seems to him that as long as *it* stands, *he* stands.

Above the dark buildings behind it, Rigshospitalet, the State Hospital, looms like a beast of prey, waiting to gobble up the weak and dying—and to help those capable of surviving to survive. And to the left, his favorite: a neon chicken, mounted five stories up on the top floor of an apartment building, laying neon eggs. The light sequence gives the illusion of movement: First the chicken appears, yellow in the dusk, with a red head and feet, then a large red egg drops, hangs at an angle on the wall, a smaller blue one drops on top of that and finally a tiny white one atop the heap. The great red egg hangs suspended above the frozen lake, reflected in the cold black surface; the chicken's red head turns to view its art before, in the wink of an eye, egg and chicken both disappear into darkness. Then the process begins again with a neon note of praise for the eggs of Irma's supermarket.

Bluett steers his course between the two cherished artifacts, monolith and egg, around the frozen island, toward the Café Front Page on the opposite embankment.

Chill seeps up from the ice through the thin soles of his shoes, penetrates his socks. He pictures thin ice cracking beneath his feet, the icy plunge, black grimy water in his eyes, his lambskin coat dragging him down as he claws toward the dark surface and all the ghosts of the dead lovers and lepers, drunks and killers, bankrupt and disgraced who took their lives here in Black Dam Lake reach up to his feet, his ankles, drawing him down to their encampment in the black cold watery room beneath the ice.

Tightening the fur collar around his throat, he whispers aloud in Danish, *"Jeg går ud til Sortedamsø,"* a Danish proverb of sorts: *I'll go out to Black Dam Lake,* something like *Good-bye, cruel world, down the flusher.*

He steps up onto the opposite embankment, tries to stamp warmth back into his soles, crosses to the Café Front Page, nearly empty at this hour, despite the fact that *l'heure bleue* comes charitably early at this parallel in winter. Eyeglasses steaming and nose running in the sudden warmth, he strips off his coat and scarf and gloves and Kangol, mops nose and lenses with a clean white handkerchief, and proceeds to the bar.

An indifferent barmaid, heartbreakingly slender, looks at him without speaking.

He smiles at her, cheerfully says, "Hej!" Then, "Double Stolichnaya on the rocks," he says in Danish. "No fruit."

She squints with incomprehension. He points at the bottle. She scoops ice into a glass with her slender red fingers, pours the vodka into a pewter measure, once, twice. Four centiliters, hardly enough to fill his hollow tooth. He likes the fact that her bare fingers touched his ice cubes, would kiss them if allowed to.

"Introibo ad altare dei," intones Bluett.

She peers at him. *"Hvad for noget?"* she says. "What for something?" Danish idiom.

He shakes his head with a smile, pays, takes a bamboo-mounted newspaper from the rack and sits by the window where he can watch the street, the lake and the interior of the café all at once. He raises his drink, relishing the chill damp glass against his palm and fingers.

"To god," he mutters, being the only customer in the place, tastes, sighs. "The joy of my youth." He tastes again, sets the glass down.

He is looking at a newspaper, *BT*, a late-morning Copenhagen tabloid, and it makes him think of Francesca, whom he met through a personal ad in that newspaper, just after he and Jette split. Her ad was one line of a poem, unattributed—"*If I were tickled by the rub of love*"—and a name, Francesca, and post box. He wrote out another line from the Dylan Thomas poem, "*Rehearsing heat upon a raw-edged nerve*," and signed it Blue Patrick and his e-mail address.

A moment passes now when he thinks of what happened between Francesca and him, and he pictures himself face in hands, head beneath a pillow, dying dead and gone, put out, snuffed. Why does he feel that way? Nothing so bad happened. Nothing bad at all really. Well, a little bad. They exchanged e-mails for a month, fell in electronic love, not yet in chemical love. She was a professor of literature in Odense, a little younger than he, and they finally met. She proposed renting a suite in the Hotel Scandinavia, and they would meet in the living room of the suite, drink a bottle of champagne and see if they wanted to proceed into the bedroom. She confessed that she wanted him to tell her to undress while he just sat there in the living room, watching her evaluatingly.

When he let himself into the suite, she was already there, seated in an armchair, and he knew at once that he did not want to go farther and saw in her eyes that she did and that she saw in his eyes, in his posture, that he did not. But he pretended. He thought perhaps he could get past the first impression. They drank the champagne. By tacit agreement, they skipped her fantasy of his ordering her to undress. They went into the bedroom and undressed one another—how falsely he pretended—and made love, no *screwed*, actually it was more technical than a screw, and afterward he sat on the edge of the bed and looked at her toes. They were so stubbed, and all of his pretense must have been translucent at that moment, for she began to weep, and all masks were down. She knew and he knew and it seemed such a moment of frailty, of the frailty of affection, that whenever after he thought of her, he had that reaction of wanting to bury his face in his hands and his head beneath a pillow. For shame. For sorrow. For not wanting her when she wanted him. For the thinness of his pretense.

This is not a good thing to be thinking on a Friday night, he thinks, and while the sound system plays Buddy Holly singing about how easy it is to fall in love, he turns to the *BT* and leafs through it at a leisurely pace. The front page story is about a seventeen-year-old Russian boy, son of an immigrant family, who killed his father with an ax while the man sat in his chair and watched television. The boy's two younger brothers stood by with knives prepared to intervene in case the coup should fail, and three sisters and the mother huddled in the kitchen. The boy was found guilty but received no sentence because the father, it came out in the trial, had been a mad sadist who had tormented his family for all their lives. In the mornings they were compelled to rise in silence, bathe, dress, and sit silently in their assigned places at the breakfast table until the father sat and gave the nod that they could begin to eat and speak. Sometimes he made them wait on his pleasure for an hour. If they did not comply, they were whipped, punched, kicked, threatened with death. It seems the father was a jovial man in public. All this occurred in secret, within the family walls.

Bluett turns the page, sips his vodka, orders peanuts which the gloomy barmaid delivers without a word, takes his ten-crown coin silently.

He reads an item about a pig farmer who is suing the state because he has lost more than fifty percent of his hearing from the constant pig screams. He is a state contractor, so feels the state must compensate him.

Another, heartier draught of spirits and he proceeds to an article about a freak hailstorm in Dublin. The article includes background research on hail. "Like tumors," it says, "hailstones come in standard sizes: the size of a pea, a walnut, a golf ball, a pool ball, a baseball, a grapefruit. There are even cases on record of cars totalled by hailstones, of light aircraft whose fabric was torn to rags, of cattle killed out on the open range, leaking their bespattered brains into the ground." Bluett rereads the last sentence to be certain it actually says that; it does. The Dublin hail had decimated a flock of pigeons on O'Connell Street; a dozen dead birds were found outside the post office.

On the next page he reads an article about the Hale-Bopp comet accompanied by a map with flow arrows showing where it will be visible when. He writes behind his ear (as the Danes say) that it should soon be clearly displayed in the northern sky above the lake here.

He drains his glass. The slushy ice chills his teeth. He calls to the barmaid for another just as the door opens and his friend Sam Finglas floats in.

"Sam!"

The man halts and looks about with his startled blue eyes. He has a dreamy look about him. Then, with a visible reluctance that wounds Bluett, "Hey, Blue," he says mildly.

"You been over to Christiania smoking some of that hippie hay or something? You look spaced."

Sam chuckles, and Bluett notices the man's clothes: a Pierre Cardin black glove-leather coat he hasn't seen before, with a padded, leather-trimmed vest under it, black shirt and burnt-sienna silk tie under an elegant bottle-green cashmere sweater. The waitress delivers Bluett's vodka and waits to be paid, eyeing Sam's coat.

"Join me in the sacrament," Bluett says to his friend.

"Can't, Blue. Got an appointment."

"An *appointment*? You dog. Is that who you're all cleaned up for?"

Sam grins self-deprecatingly.

"That's a delicious coat," the barmaid says, her fingers trailing affection-ately over the leather on Sam's chest, and Bluett is jealous. He tips her, gets no thanks, says to Sam as she disappears, "Well, what in the hell are you here for if you're not drinking?"

"Just a quick one, then." He goes to the bar, and Bluett watches him chatting with the girl there. She smiles brilliantly as she takes his money, and he returns with a bottle of snow beer.

Bluett says, "My feel-good shield has suffered a few blows."

Sam's startled eyes show lack of comprehension. Bluett drops it, though he can't help but wonder about himself in comparison to Sam. "So tell me about this *appointment*." They raise their glasses, say, "*Skål, slanté, kipis,*" sip. Bluett adds, "*Terviseks,*" an Estonian toast, in honor of the madman who had accosted him in Vesterbro the previous week.

"Just an appointment," Sam says through a cryptic smile.

"You've gotten lucky. What do you have that I don't? Don't answer. Other than that fantastic coat? Be careful. Your brothers'll hit you on the head and throw you in a ditch."

Sam takes a long draft of his beer while Bluett sits watching the white snowflakes imprinted on the blue label of the bottle.

Sam lowers his glass, sighs. "Tell you, Blue: this woman rings the bell. Never thought this would happen again. Again? Hell, never happened before. Never really wanted it to. But here it is. Happening. It's like . . . you hold back, you hold back, and suddenly . . ." He shakes his head, baffled.

"You surrender," Bluett says, thinking he's completing Sam's thought.

The startled eyes. "What do you mean?"

"You surrender. You know, you give in to the, uh, the calling of love. Or some such."

"Yeah," Sam breathes. "Yeah, like that."

Bluett laughs. "You got bit bad, my friend!"

The startled eyes flash, blue glass. "You got something better going?"

Bluett raises his hands. "Hey, no offense, I'm nowhere. I'm jealous." He thinks again of Benthe and wonders why he doesn't want that. But he doesn't.

Sam's eyes are earnest again. "Listen. You live a life that is all, like, broken up. Compartmentalized. I don't mean *you*, I mean people. Like the Brits say: One. It don't have to be that way." He sighs, abandoning the enormity of explaining himself.

"You gonna marry the chick or pay her off?"

The eyes flash again, then damp down. "No. Don't know. Hardly really know her to say it like it is. Yet, anyway." He burps discreetly behind his fist.

Bluett thinks maybe this explains why the barmaid was drawn in. The second law of Bluett: When a man has one woman, other women want him, too. The first law is: No woman wants a womanless man. *Hell, when I was married . . .*, Bluett thinks and pauses in thought. *You were fucking miserable.*

Sam leans closer across the table, speaks softly. "She is wild. She wants to do it all. She really *wants* it. And she's fun. And my god is she beautiful!"

I'll be the judge of that, Bluett thinks. "Who is she?"

"She's Russian. A blonde, blonde Russian. Funny, I used to read Russian lit in college, loved it. Jesus. Dostoyevsky. Turgenev. Tolstoy. Chekhov. And of course Nabokov. Hell, it's like this was ordained, awaiting me somehow. And now I got the woman, I'm not interested in the books.

Look, I'm what? Seven–eight years older than you, Blue? My age, never thought it could be like this."

"So, you gonna marry her?"

He shrugs. "When Karine and I split. All that, that, that mess. No. Don't want it no more. See people get divorced, then marry again. Come on, get real, you know? You been through it now too, you must know what I mean. A harpy ex. The confused kids."

"My kids are okay," Bluett says. "Took some time, but . . ."

"So you're the exception. But you know, when I want to be with her, I call, she says, come on overrr, with those sexy rolling Ruski r's. I mean, I visit her . . ." He hesitates, looks embarrassed to say what he is about to say, but is clearly too eager to share it. "I go over, she lets me in . . ." His voice lowers. "She kneels down and takes off my fuckin' shoes, man! I mean this woman is *beautiful*, and she's young, and she kneels down and takes off my *shoes*! And . . ." He wants to tell more, Bluett can see, but drinks some beer instead, and Bluett can see that he is not going to get the rest of it. "She understands me. She's a *genius*," he adds suddenly. "An emotional genius. It's like she *knows* me, you know, like no one ever has . . ." He stops, as though he has suddenly heard himself gushing and feels embarrassed.

"Is she bright like in the brain as well as the heart? Is she wise as she is fair?"

"Wisdom of the pussy, Blue," he says and looks surprised at himself for saying it, but goes on. "Wish I could crawl in and *die* there. I would light a candle to her cunt and worship it."

"Is this love or a hard-on? Not that anything's wrong with a stiff. I presume you didn't mean literally die."

Sam's eyes look as though they're someplace else, seeing something else. "She just *knows* me."

"Sounds like maybe she's in love with you, Sam. Isn't she gonna want more?"

"That's the thing. She says, however I want it. She wants it that way, too."

"Aren't, uh, East European women usually a little more, I don't know, down to earth, *materialism* wise?"

"Not this one, buddy."

Bluett fills his mouth with vodka, lets it chill his tongue before he swallows. "I've made plenty of mistakes in my life, but I've also learned a couple things. One is when a woman wants to give me that much it's because, regardless what she says, she either loves me, with all the implications and expectations that involves, or she wants something out of me. Or both. Maybe one and the same." Bluett tries to think a little more about what he is trying to say, but what had seemed very clear when he began suddenly blurs in his mind. He wonders what he is talking about. Is he jealous and trying to bring Sam down? Or what? He feels embarrassed at having said so much, asked questions. He thinks again of telling Sam about Benthe, the threesome, but he realizes abruptly that the reason he doesn't tell is because he just plain didn't enjoy it. It was pretense. Like with Francesca.

He sips his vodka, decides to turn it all into a joke. "It's like the old Japanese proverb, Sam. If you want to keep a woman, make her pay. A woman will never leave you while you owe her something."

Sam just nods, lost in his own thoughts. He says, "I met her at a party." He lowers his voice again. "Dancing with her, right? We just met, talked a little. Clearly fucking hitting it off, right? So I ask her to dance a slow one, Smokey Robinson, and her lips are up against my ear, warm breath, and whispers . . ." He looks right and left, behind him, leans closer. "'I vant to suck your cock.'" Sam's face is alight. "Just like that: *I vant to suck your cock!*"

"Hey, take it easy, man, you're gettin' me excited, slow down, no, where do you find parties where you meet women like that, huh? Where?" But all the while he is play-acting to be kind to Sam and thinking about Benthe and wondering.

Sam is chuckling as he lifts his glass, drains off the rest of his beer. "Woman ever say a thing like that to you?"

"Yeah, *once*, a hooker." He sees hurt in Sam's eyes and realizes he wanted to cut him down a notch, so he hastens to placate. "No, seriously, Sam, so when do I get to meet her?"

Sam's smile slips away. He stares off a little. "This is kind of separate like. Separate part of my life, you know? For now."

"Scared of the competition, huh?"

The distant eyes turn to Bluett, slowly refocus in a grin. "Eat your liver, boy!" He tips back his glass to let the last drops of beer slide into his mouth, sets it down with a clack. "Got to go."

"Hey, watch out for the old ticker, huh?" Bluett says. "And watch you don't use up all your orgasms. Limited number coming to us, you know. According to the L.O.T.—the Limited Orgasm Theory."

Sam is at the door, buttoning his fancy leather coat, a merry smile beneath his startled blue eyes. He lifts his left hand like Hitler, and cold air sweeps in as he departs.

Bluett watches him move quickly up to Queen Louise's Bridge, toward the city center. Then he sits looking at the white snowflakes on the blue label of the empty beer bottle. He looks into his glass. The ice is slush, a finger left. He glances out at the lake again, glimpses Sam's head bobbing along above the bridge wall, looks across the dark sweep of ice to the lights on the other side. And he realizes why he doesn't want Benthe: because when he got to know her, he realized he couldn't love her. The chemistry was not right. She was too . . . Abruptly he realizes he doesn't have to understand it. It simply is how he feels.

Behind the bar, the girl leans on her elbows, staring at a glass of water.

"Dead tonight, huh?" he says.

She lifts her eyes to him, lifts her brow, says nothing.

Would a kind word kill ya? Bluet spills the rest of the vodka down his throat, goes to the gent's. He studies himself in the mirror over the sink. His once grand lambskin coat has gone a bit shabby, scuffed up, missing a button, some loose threads hanging from the seam. He looks at his Marimekko shirt, notices its collar-lapels are washed out, and at his tie and sweater, his winter-gray face, wonders what he wants, considers taking on some more translation jobs, maybe buy some new clothes, attend some translator conferences, meet some new people. Maybe he should put an ad in the papers, personal. Saying what?

Man, white, advanced youth, divorced, children, has no idea
what he wants, seeks great-looking, bright, like-minded woman,
object unknown, but chemistry must be right.

He considers going home to read a book, or to watch a video—maybe get out all the movies Bernard Herrmann did the music for, *The Wrong Man*, *Citizen Kane*, *Vertigo*, *Psycho*, *Fahrenheit 451*, *Taxi Driver* . . . He shakes his head, winks at himself in the mirror, polishes his glasses—he wants to have fun tonight!—steps out, crosses to the door, raising his arm to the barmaid. "*Hej hej*," he calls out.

"*Hej hej*," she replies, but somehow it sounds more like *Fuck off, jerk*. Chemistry wasn't right.

At Kruts Karport, he eats a bowl of chili, and he feels okay, studies the green row of absinthe bottles behind the bar, 136 proof, resists the urge, orders a glass of wine. He looks into a local newspaper to avoid looking at the tables full of beery youngsters in sweaters and leather jeans, grinning and pawing each other.

Then he is surreptitiously watching a man alone at a corner table, perhaps a dozen years his senior, Sam's age maybe, little older, drinking a pint of beer. The man lights a cigar, and from a satchel on the table removes a book and begins to read. Bluett cranes discreetly to see the title. *Finnegans Wake*. Considers calling across to the man, but what? Something about James Joyce. Then the door opens, a woman in a long green woolen coat enters, eyes the green of her coat and smile so light. She crosses to the man, who looks up just in time to receive a kiss on his mouth from her pretty lips. They appear to be about the same age, couple of notches short of sixty maybe, but still youthful, like where Bluett wants to be at their age, and the way their eyes meet, their smiles, touches pleasurable yearning in Bluett. *Could happen to you. That old chemistry.*

Relieved he hadn't spoken to the man, he has another glass of wine, tips the charming, pretty, round-faced young waitress whose name, he happens to know, is Cirkeline and who rewards him with a smile meant for him only. He pastes it to his feel-good shield and sets off past Silver Square to Nørreport, down Fiolstræde, past the university, the cathedral, behind which people queue at a yellow-lit sausage wagon on the dark street to eat steaming pølser with their cold bare fingers. Through Jorck's Passage, he takes a left on Strøget and cuts across alongside the Round Tower, looks into Café Rex—and remembers a British woman he met there once who invited him home to her tiny apartment into which was crammed a white baby grand piano and who allowed him to undress her to her white lace garters, which, when he saw them, instantly caused him to go down on her. He strolls along Pilegården, continues down to the Palæ Bar on New Nobility Street, stands on the dark sidewalk, looking into the bright window at the crowded tables, decides to save that for later, doubles back for a peek into the Bo-Bi Bar.

Across the half-filled bar room, he spots a familiar face at the back table, two familiar faces. An American translator and an Irish book salesman. The Irishman waves him over. Dermot Cleary, with a face full of whisky veins, map of Ireland on his nose. Bluett notes they are drinking Black Gold beer and Gammel Dansk bitters, orders a round and three hard-boiled eggs on his way back to them. Dermot has channeled a series of lucrative contracts his way in the past couple of years and Bluett feels he owes him.

Watching their fingers fumble at the brown bits of eggshell, Bluett sees they are a few rounds up on him, reminds himself Dermot has supplied a good deal of his business in the past year. He wonders if the American resents Dermot's generosity to Bluett. He is a southern Californian who jumped ship and made his way to Sweden during the sixties to beat a tour in Vietnam, then moved to Denmark, which is a NATO member, previously off limits, when Jimmy Carter let all ship-jumpers off the hook. But the American—Milt Sever—is listening raptly to the story Dermot is telling about a Danish poet who has just returned from Brazil where, Dermot reports, the writer has reported to him in considerable detail that he had paid children to have sex with him.

Bluett cracks his egg on the edge of the table and rolls it between his palms, peels away the shell in one crackling sheet, pinches on finger salt from a stone bowl on the table.

"You wouldn't actually consider such a thing yourself, would you, Dermot?" he hears himself ask and regrets being there.

Dermot blushes, clearly surprised. "I but tell the tale that I heard told," he says and looks at Milt Sever. "What about yourself, Milt? Would you ever consider such a thing yourself?"

Milt's smile is buttery. He is a tall, broad-shouldered, dark-haired man. He clearly enjoys looking at Bluett in light of what he is about to say.

"Well, now, I'm sure I would hate myself in the morning, but . . ." He shrugs serenely. Bluett is surprised to find himself having to resist the urge to take a swing at the smug mouth, realizes he would probably miss or be blocked and find himself engaged in a humiliating and ridiculous tussle, realizes he is in danger of screwing himself out of money, a lot of money, and hears himself say, "Well, I think a man ought to burn in hell's river of boiling blood for a thing like that." He holds his breath.

"You're an honorable fellow," says Dermot, and Bluett starts calculating an exit that might cut his losses.

But Milt is not finished with him. "Have you seen Andreas Fritzsen's new novel?" Fritzsen is a Danish-Anglo writer living and teaching in Denmark, a novelist who makes his living in the university. Bluett has read the first chapter of the man's new novel in some literary journal. It is about the brief legality of child pornography in Denmark in the late sixties and early seventies and it includes a scene in which an adult male engineers penetration with a ten-year-old child which, when Bluett read it, had inspired him to write a letter expressing distaste to *Politiken*. Bluett's letter had evoked a surprising response from people who called upon the immortal beauty of Nabokov, Genet, and others in defense of sexual love between children and adults, all of which makes Bluett realize he has walked into a trap here. He begins to prepare an argument against the stance that Humbert truly loved Lolita by pointing out that Humbert extorts sexual favors from the child in return for her allowance, but in that direction lies rage and loss of income.

He shrugs, raises his Gammel Dansk, says, "Gentlemen. I drink to your very good health," swallows, chases it with Carlsberg draft, and as he retreats from the Bo-Bi Bar, wonders whether he has ruined his economic stability. First Benthe, now Dermot.

Human beings, he thinks, *are not to traffic with. And where does that leave me?*

Moving toward Kongens Nytorv, he refuses to think about these people, takes a long loop behind the Royal Theater to see if there are any attractive joints back there. He notices then, just across from the New Scene, on the edge of the square, a scooped-away corner with a door on which is mounted a brass plate that says,

He stares, wondering, crosses the square, past the French Embassy to Nyhavn. *Your problem,* he thinks, as he climbs down the steps into the half-basement of the Mermaid Bar, *is a classic one: Lackanookie. Well, not exactly lackanookie, but lackalove-nookie. Forget these provincial fools. Have fun until you meet someone who has the chemistry.*

Here he continues with beer, orders a pint of draft lager and sits on a stool at one of the high drum tables. The place is filling up. A fiftyish Scot in the middle of the room strums a guitar and sings "The Streets of London," as Bluett surveys the joint. No familiar faces.

The Scot takes a break, and an Italian kid comes on who is much smoother. He sings some Simon and Garfunkel, Elton John—"Benny and the Jets," a favorite of Bluett's. The first pint goes down fast, and half-way through his second, the bar continues to fill nicely. The pleasure of a crowded bar is that it forces contact. Three women join him at his drum table. Look like office girls maybe. He likes the blonde. They chat a bit in Danish. She asks him about his accent, asks how an American speaks such good Danish. He tells her she's too kind, explains his ex-wife was Danish, the key word being *ex*, his ringless fingers resting on the table. He buys a round. More people come in, forcing them closer together. She lights a cigarette. "Is it okay I am smoking near you?"

"Sure," he says, wishing he were upwind.

The Italian kid is singing "Nothing's gonna change my world" and doing a fair job of it. Bluett studies the blonde woman's face. She is maybe thirty-two, very full-lipped with a bright smile and light eyes. Her lips are rouged pink and he cannot take his eyes off them. They talk about films, music. She buys a round. *Nice habit for a woman.* She tells him that she lives in Albertslund.

Shit.

She glances at her watch. He guesses that she's thinking about the train schedule. Her girlfriends have moved to another table. Her name is Birgitte. The last time he looked at his watch it was nearly eleven P.M.

Their glasses are full again, and he is shoulder to shoulder with her, the wall behind them, staring into her light, bright eyes. He kisses her full pink lips, tastes her tongue. Then she kisses him. Kisses and smiles in the dim smoky light, hands touching. Soft lips. Soft. And she surprises him by sucking on his tongue. Quite briskly. The Italian kid takes a break and the Scot comes on again with "The Streets of London." The girlfriends are back, and Birgitte has to go, to get the train. She writes her name and phone number on a coaster, which he slips into his pocket. She gives him a last lingering tongue kiss to catch his attention, stands for a moment pressing her breasts against his arm, smiling at him, then she waves good-bye with a cute tiny circular movement of her palm.

Bluett sits there watching a snow-beer poster above the taps. The white flakes really seem to be falling down the night-blue background. He watches, hypnotized, realizes he is getting sloshed and likes it. It occurs to him once again that love is a chemical. Incredible but true. His beer is nearly empty. The Scot seems to believe that he is the vicar of Roger Whittaker in Copenhagen. Bluett takes the coaster out of his pocket, reads what she has printed there. *Birgitte Svane. Svane means swan in Danish*, he thinks. *Maybe she and I would give birth to Helen.* She had told him she was a bookkeeper at the electric works near Nørreport. She had a two-year-old daughter named Astrid. Sweet name. A little girl. Bluett has nothing against little kids. Likes them. But *Albertslund.* The chemistry was good but the geography was way off.

Bluett has been to Albertslund two times in his life, the first and the last. Middle of nowhere. If hell was absence, as Thomas Aquinas or some such philosopher suggested, Albertslund was a good candidate for hell. Nothing. Nowhere. He had suggested she stay the night with him, here, which was possibly some kind of somewhere, a lesser hell at least, and she had smiled, as if to consider it for a moment, then had said, "Call me."

Nice answer.

But I will never visit you in Albertslund. Ever.

The Scot sings "The Streets of London" yet again. Bluett wonders if the man is having a nervous breakdown. Two American women sit at the table beside his, drinking dark beer.

"It's so rich and creamy!" the one exclaims as though she is in the grips of ecstasy, not of a pharmaceutical sort. He empties his beer and climbs out to the street, the cold clean air along the frozen canal. He looks down into it. The old sailing boats moored there are frozen into the ice. He sees an empty wine bottle frozen to the surface, upside down, the husk of a leftover New Year's Eve rocket.

There are many people on the street. Nearly midnight. He begins to walk, feeling good, past Tattoo Jack's, hears a singer through a bar door singing, "Kiss my neck! Watch me ride!" Or maybe it's "Watch me slide." He passes Skipperkroen, Pakhus, Færgekroen, Gilleleje, all packed and noisy, some in a semibasement, some up the steps, these harbor streets that years ago were the sailor's district, now sequestered by the bourgeoisie.

He climbs the steps of one lively joint where a crowd is gathered around three guitarists in the smoky back. The singer is doing "Wonderful Tonight" as Bluett orders a beer, looks around at the men and women in the smoky light, thinks *The night life ain't no good life but it's my life*, savoring the moment, the image of a slender woman standing there alone swaying to the music. The beer is very cold and tastes wonderful.

Perhaps it is the next or the one after that but suddenly it begins to taste acidic. The musicians do a last number, then a last encore, an absolute last one, "The House of the Rising Sun," and Bluett gets up to let himself out while the music is still going rather than having to leave a dead place, but before he gets to the door the music stops and the juke goes on, someone singing, "Kiss my neck . . ." Must be some new hit.

The streets are still full of people. He stands outside for a moment watching them, pleasantly buzzed, charged by Birgitte's kisses. Those lips. *That was really something, young woman wanted to suck on my tongue like that.* Still a little attraction value in the old forty-deuce fart. But I'll never visit her in Albertslund. *Never.*

Twenty yards up the canal, something catches his eye. A fancy leather coat. Sam Finglas.

Bluett opens his mouth to call out, then notices Finglas is walking with someone, a woman. An incredibly beautiful woman, pale, hair long, light as white gold, high cheekbones, slightly Asian cast to her face, stacked soles with even higher heels, stilettos, beneath the hem of her light fur coat. And Bluett realizes how buzzed he is because it takes a moment for him to recognize that this is the Russian woman Sam talked about. He stands there on the step, open-mouthed, breathing steam. They are coming sideways toward him before they turn toward Kongens Nytorv, and Bluett catches a full view of her. She is as tall as Sam and slender. She moves like a song, and her eyes are blue as ice, her skin white, her mouth wide, lips inviting as a plum.

He closes his mouth and follows at a distance, unable to resist. Sam has his arm around her shoulder, and her head is tipped onto his. They cross the square toward the Royal Theater, past the statue of the mounted king in the center, and on the other side, they stop in front of a door. She rings the bell. A moment later the door opens, and they enter.

Standing on the opposite sidewalk, he feels like a voyeur, staring through a keyhole at a door: *the Satin Club*.

He considers following them in, ringing the bell. Then he peers down beneath his fog of drink at the muddy brown toes of his shoes and sees he should not, walks home along the teeming Copenhagen streets.

It is a thirty-minute walk to the lakes. Good exercise. Past groups of people, couples, the scattered lone wolf, staggering. Two A.M. Some big-faced kid yells at him, his stomach plunges, he keeps moving.

Along the lakes, the street is deserted and dark, the frozen water streaked silver in the moonlight, most of the windows on the other side blackened. Just the neon chicken, the neon eggs dropping, the red neon chicken head turning to see the product of its work, then nothing again.

A taxi flies past, green dome light lit. He finds himself thinking about his kids, when they were little, when they were a family. How he misses those years. Family. A point in time is all. There and gone. He is proud of them, both off to university, doing well. Maudlin thoughts assail him there, thinking of his wife and how he never managed to make her happy, even as much as he wanted to, as much as he tried, even if she would not agree with him that he had tried. For that matter, did *she* try to make *him* happy? Two-way street there. Mexican standoff.

Suddenly he misses his father, aware of the burden of fatherhood, wishes his father were here so he could tell him he understood that it had been hard for him, that he had not understood that before.

He thinks of all the years in Denmark, speaking a foreign tongue, which he is good at, but nonetheless to him is like wandering through a misty landscape, finding the words, but more slowly, rarely one hundred percent sure where you are, never quite at home here. Never quite at home in the States anymore, either. He thinks of a book he read as a kid, *The Man Without a Country*, a man torn between the U.S. and England in the early years; he recalls it ending with the man on a raft out in the ocean by himself, not allowed in either place anymore. The image is very sharp in his memory. Then he remembers that is because in fact he did not read the book, he read the classic comic and that was the drawing on the cover.

He crosses Queen Louise's Bridge, pauses in the shadows, and the sweep of the moonlit ice finds his heart. He mocks himself for a self-pitying fool. This is a beautiful place. He has nothing to regret. All he has to do is translate five pages a day and he can survive. Simple enough. What a deal. No boss. No annoying office intrigues. He has it made. He thinks fleetingly of Dermot Cleary and Benthe and wonders if he has fucked himself out of a flow of work, thinks, *Ah fuck it, fuck it all.*

He blows his nose, moves on, remembering how when he was a kid, fifteen, eighteen, in his early twenties, he yearned for a woman, desperate to be complete. Missing a girl and trying to make it real, to make it mean something, excite him, but he was only exciting himself. He is not quite certain what he means with that thought, thinking again of kissing Birgitte Svane in the bar, the healing touch of her mouth, her fingertips on his cheek, in the close-cut hair at the base of his skull, her sweet spearmint tongue.

All my life, he thinks, *decade after decade, I ask myself is it really true, am I deluded, can this be a fact? But decade after decade, my eye, my heart, my body tell me the most beautiful thing in this world is to see a woman walk, to see a woman, to look in a woman's eyes, kiss a woman's mouth. What I am to do with her and what it is all about I do not know. I used to think it was sex, to fuck, but it is not really that at all.* It is to touch, share a moment. He remembers moments with his wife over all their years together and feels unreal to think they are apart, that their life together failed. But it did. And that's that.

At his building he pushes through the unlocked blue street door, climbs the stairs to his first-floor apartment, glances across the hall at Sam

Finglas's door. He'll get married, you watch. They'll move. That apartment is not big enough for a couple. Who could resist a woman who looks like that if she is all the things he spoke about? Sam is his closest friend in Denmark. Another departure.

He lets himself in to his apartment and sits in the armchair without taking off his coat. He feels that his vision is dimming, his stomach hurts. He feels he is dying.

Fuck that.

He rises, sheds his coat, pours a glass of vodka on three rocks, and turns a straight-back chair, back to the window, straddles the seat and looks out across the lake. A lone couple is walking, arm in arm, across the silver-lit ice, silhouettes moving on the frozen water.

Sometimes when he thinks about the fact that this life might be all we have, nothing but a growing accumulation of memories that will end in the wall of death and vanish, sometimes when he thinks that this is all there is and all that will be, that it will all be over just like that, the life of his childhood, his parents, his own children's childhood, all of them done with, he feels he is locked in a small windowless room and that he must break out, must try to break out and that he must do everything, anything, yet that too, all of it is doomed to the same end, vanishing, and all the while, every minute trickles away, the sun burns consuming itself, and we are without power, alone, kissing in some smoky room listening to some cheap music before we die . . .

Rising, he reaches to the CD player, locates Miles's *Aura*, slots it into the machine, presses play, backs up to his armchair, sits, hears Miles's trumpet, John McLaughlin's guitar, the strange fusion symphony of jazz, rock, contemporary "serious" music, lowers his eyelids, listening, but lifts them again just as the "Electric Red" cut begins.

He raises his glass, looks through it at the neon chicken, the neon egg that seems to drop, its red reflection smeared across the silver-black ice of the lake, seeming enclosed in Miles's "Electric Red" horn blares, and Bluett thinks of all the lovers down there beneath the surface in their freezing black room.

4. A Night in Tunisia

Bluett opens his eyes to see patterned on the wall the light cast by a streetlamp through the slats of the windowblinds. Still dark. He lies on the narrow bed listening to the thump thump of little feet in the apartment upstairs, waits for signs of a hangover to move in his blood, but feels nothing.

However, if he sits up, he suspects, pain will begin to migrate within the tender walls of his skull. He puts it off, staring at the egg-white ceiling high above his head. From time to time the air splits with the shriek of a machine, a lathe perhaps, something that cuts metal, some industrious person out back somewhere working to improve his rooms. The ceiling is clear as an empty screen. The flies are gone, dead or hibernating for the winter, or planted as eggs somewhere. In summer there are always a few flies flitting around beneath the ceiling, at the top of the tall window. He lies here sometimes and watches them, and they seem so pointless, so very pointless that they are almost friends, seem like friends, kindred creatures, black specks floating beneath a blank white ceiling. He misses their presence now.

He tries to guess the time. No music emanates from the Kingo Institute of Dance for Children next door so it is not yet ten. Nor can he hear Miss Kingo's barked commands. Yet the dark is not nighttime dense. He guesses eight A.M., reaches for his watch. Close to eight. The movement brings no pain. He remembers Birgitte from Albertslund, those lips, that sweet tongue, reaches under the blanket, considers, then heaves the covers back and swings out of bed. Out in the living room he does fifty push-ups on the dusty carpet, sneezes and rolls over on his back panting, staring up through the window, through the lacework of bare walnut branches to the dark blue winter sky and the still-bright globe of moon behind the tree.

How to use this virgin day?

He could translate, get ahead of himself, extra five pages. There are two projects on his desk—an *instructions for use* for a turnkey summer-house rental plan and a museum catalog for a porcelain exhibit. He is stuck half-way through the summer-house instructions. Something about the shower. It says, *Du er nødt til at fange dråberne når de er der.* Literally: *You have to catch the drops when they are there.* Meaning, he presumes, something like: *The shower does not always function optimally. If it doesn't work, try again.* No, not quite. He's not certain the Danish sentence is valid. Maybe written by a foreigner, translated from a bad translation from the Japanese. His temples throb.

No translation today. Take your Saturday as a day of rest, of play.

He considers calling Benthe. He's horny. Got the hangover horns. She's so goddamn sexy. But that's a can of worms, and he finally got the toothpaste back in the tube by lying to her, telling her he had a girlfriend, so why try to open it again. He thinks of calling the woman with the white lace garter belt, but he can remember neither her name nor precisely where she lives. Simplest thing is to have a honeymoon of the hand. *Up like a skyrocket, down like a stick.*

The sky is now a paler blue but the moon is still visible, and the sun has not yet reddened the tops of the trees or the upper windows across the lake. He thinks of crawling back into bed, does sit-ups, staring up at the white ceiling, until he can do no more, and lies back breathing heavily, his forehead and back clammy with sweat.

This is good for you, he thinks. *To suffer.*

Something makes him think of Sam Finglas, that door, the Satin Club, that woman. He remembers Birgitte's light eyes, her mouth. He gets up and looks for his coat, finds it slung across the armchair, and in the pocket the coaster with her number on it. The moon is just over the tops of the buildings across the lake now. There is an icing of white frost on the street and roadway, on parked cars and on the frozen lake.

The moon has grown paler in the sky. He drinks a glass of tomato juice and imagines another night in the bars listening to a jowly Scot trying to imitate Roger Whittaker singing the bloody streets of bloody fucking London.

Hour be damned. He picks up the phone and keys in Birgitte's number. It rings eight times before it clicks off, unanswered. He taps out the number again, carefully. No answer.

He feels stupid, wonders if she gave him a phoney number. But why? He didn't ask for it. It was her idea. He tries again, gets a sleepy woman's voice, asks for Birgitte and is told she is spending the weekend with her mother in Odense. Which makes no sense, but he hangs up and looks out the window to see the red tint of sunlight on the treetops and roofs. He does another set of push-ups, needs something, music. *Aura* is still in the CD player. He punches the button to start it and makes a cup of Nescafé, which he drinks at the window, allowing the strange compelling swells of sound from Miles's horn to sweep over his body. He watches a rook walk along a benchtop on the lake bank below, a jogger moving swiftly along the opposite side, a flash of gulls lift from the ice.

His gaze fixes on the tilted monolith, the Peace Gate, frozen in its fall. Now there are two rooks, facing each other with bowed heads. A blonde girl passes, walking a black-and-white cocker, and the sunlight has made its way to the red brick on the other side. A couple jogs past in fuchsia sweats.

He wants to get out. Get showered, get dressed, get out! Thinking of a place to go, he gathers some copies of old *New Yorker*s, one of his self-indulgences, and finds a plastic bag to carry them in.

Grateful for his legs, his feet, which carry him briskly along Webersgade, beside the many-colored faces of its narrow row houses, across Silver Square, past the Café Under the Clock, into the open gate of the Botanical Garden, diagonally across through the barren winter trees and bushes, each labeled neatly in Danish and Latin. Bluett cannot retain the names. He is aware that he sees trees and bushes, even flowers, generically mostly.

No, he can remember every tree and bush and flower in the garden that he shared with his ex and his children for all those years in the Brønshøj house, by the moor, until he became invisible in his own house. Not to the kids. Never to the kids. To the ex. First there were her years of rage. At what? Bluett thinks she raged only at herself, but is aware that he cannot see his own face, his own being. Who knows what he did, what provocations he was guilty of? He only knew love was gone, if there had ever been love in the first place (and what, indeed, *is* love—never solved that question), and then she was raging—over everything, anything— that the Christmas tree was not straight. Every single twenty-third of December, same thing: *You Irish slob! You can't do anything right because you don't care, because you don't see, you are not aware of anything but your own fat sloppy ass . . .*

Then the rages burned out and were replaced by chill, and then he grew invisible to her, and he only waited for his boy and his girl to start university to remove himself.

Now he steps briskly along the dirt path of the Botanical Garden and remembers with rue the pleasures of the little garden in his home above the moor for all those years and the vegetation that with the rolling seasons became part of him. First the white snowbells and yellow eranthis, tiny blooms in the short, sparse, straw-colored grass. Then the crocus, orange and purple little bulbs of deep color. Then the bowed heads of the yellow daffodils and the upright tulips—the bulbs he'd purchased on business trips to Amsterdam—many colors, purple, green, red, yellow, but he loved the Queen of the Night most, so purple it was almost black. And then the grass thickened and turned a young green and the forsythia bloomed, overnight, like a yellow explosion. He still had a photo of his Timothy and Raffaella, at four and two, blond, the smiles of innocence with the branches of yellow forsythia slashing up behind them. Then the magnolia tree in the center of the garden with its furry buds turning to the palest lavender blooms—like lovely bloodless alabaster flesh—until the whole tree was abloom. Then the green pear blossoms and the tiny yellow mirabelles and the long, tall rose hedge blooms, red and white and yellow. And often, miraculously, the dust-ball mushrooms would appear, always in a new place, three or four of them. They would grow big as soccer balls, but he had learned the size they were tastiest—a small cantaloupe—and he would peel and slice them, fry them in butter and make a cream sauce and serve them on slices of toasted bread with glasses of chilled Riesling. Only the kids would trust his judgment enough to join him in the eating of them, and each kid would get a small glass of wine, too, while his wife grumbled and muttered that he was risking the children's health until even his son no longer dared to taste them. Bluett knew they were safe, though.

Gone now, all of it, gone as this barren cold winter garden through which he walked. But he remembered Rilke saying that a tree only *looks* dead in winter; in truth, it is gathering its force to bloom in spring. And he must believe that of himself, too: that he is gathering force to bloom again. That he does not yet know what flowers he will bear this time, but believes that they will be strong and healthy. He must believe that. He remembers a priest he met, in, of all places, a bar, an Irish bar here in Copenhagen, who quoted a Rilke line to him: *When I stare into the chasm that is myself, I see a hundred roots silently drinking . . .*

He comes out of the gardens at the corner of Øster Voldgade and Gothersgade, waits at the red light while rattling bicycles stream past, with red-nosed riders, scarves flying, then crosses to Nørreport and the Coal Square and to Skindergade. Three steps down at number 23, and he is in the Booktrader. The owner looks up from behind the counter, and a smile brightens his squat Dostoyevskian face with its patches of beard, and in the smile Bluett notices again that his eyes are blue beneath the beige dreadlocks.

"Patrick Bluett!" cries Lars, the owner, in his deep growl, and Bluett extends his right hand to shake and his left bearing his plastic-bagged offering of *New Yorker*s.

Lars takes the bag with an eager smile. "Bluett, you're my only friend!" He shuffles through the half-dozen magazines. "This will give me hours of pleasure, my friend!" Then, glancing at his watch, he asks, "Is it too early?"

"Never too early," Bluett says, and Lars brings up a bottle of Merlot from beneath the counter and two juice glasses. With the Swiss Army knife that was a gift of appreciation from Bluett, Lars expertly slits the foil from the neck of the bottle and, with another blade, screws out the cork. On the wall above his head, in large thick black letters, is a palindrome Lars created in Latin. A palindrome generally reads the same backward and forward; however, this palindrome reads the same backward, forward, and up and down as well:

NEMO
ERAM
MARE
OMEN

I was nobody. The sea was an omen.

In fact, though Lars says Bluett is his only friend, Bluett knows he has many friends, for this bookstore is the hangout of scores of people. Bluett recognizes familiar piano notes from the CD player, a bass introduction, and realizes he is listening to Bill Evans and Paul Chambers and soon will be hearing Miles and the Trane and Cannonball going into "So What," and he just tilts his head toward the CD player, and Lars says, "Isn't life wonderful," in layers of irony that lead to genuine wonder as he lifts his glass. And there, beneath the Kasper Holten erotic ceiling sculpture—a wreath of figures emerging from a book, each performing some various manner of sexual intrusion on the next figure in the wreath, all headed toward a small distant heart—there, Bluett raises his glass in response and hears the chest-deep notes of Miles saving him from loneliness, from despair.

And he engages in sporadic, desultory conversation with Lars, happily characterized by long silences during which Lars tops up the wine and Coltrane, Cannonball, and Miles top up the music.

On any given day, Bluett is likely to meet anyone in this antiquarian bookshop—artists, musicians, writers, actors, composers, translators, ornithologists, criminologists, bookbinders, sculptors, flaneurs, expats, beautiful women aging and young—but this particular day no one appears, which is perhaps as it should be. Peaceful.

In the good weather, Lars and Bluett take advantage of their vantage point in the semibasement bookshop to enjoy a strategic view of women passing the ten-foot-wide window up to the street. Lars is fond of quoting a 1940 poem by Kaj Munk, a Lutheran priest liquidated by the Gestapo in 1944 for his anti-Nazi writings and left in a roadside ditch with a bullet in the back of his head.

But the poem Lars quotes is one in which the priest declares that he wishes to be the bicycle seat of his beloved so that he could be "intimately near God's workshop's secret territory/Nirvana's polar opposite/Life's dark spring." When Munk published the poem, it was immediately attacked by critics, to whom he responded, "I write a tribute to the female sex, bliss's earthly primordial place, and instantly a pack of curs comes baying under the flag of the figleaf and praise its pornography. Go to hell! That's where you belong with your swinish thoughts!"

When Lars told Bluett that, about the response of Munk to the critics, Bluett almost wanted to join the Danish state religion.

Lars closes at two on Saturday, and Bluett eats lunch around the corner on Krystal Street, across from the synagogue, beside the main library. A couple of pints of Royal pilsner and three "unspecified" open sandwiches, deep ones served on dark rye by a pretty, smiling waitress who reminds Bluett of the British actress Babs Milligan when she was young. The place is called Café Halvvej—Café Halfway—and the name always makes Bluett think of Dante:

> *Halfway on the path of my life*
> *I went astray and found myself on a dark road*
> *For the straight way was no longer in view . . .*

The remainder of the afternoon he spends walking, to earn an appetite for dinner. Copenhagen is a city to walk in, one of the reasons he settled here. He is a walker. And he loves the serving houses, of which there are many. And the light, even in winter, when the city is a perfect noir setting, dark—in the depth of winter—from before four in the afternoon until nearly ten in the morning.

By seven o'clock, he finds himself wandering through darkness across Knippels Bridge toward Christianshavn, and he realizes that all along he has had a plan. Down from the bridge and along Torvegade, over the canal, past Christianshavn Square, he follows the plan to the Spicy Kitchen for a dinner of curried lamb and a pint of Carlsberg Classic.

By nine, after a beer and a shooter of Havana Club at the Eiffel Bar on Wilders Street, he is strolling past Our Savior's Church and along Prinsessegade toward Christiania, an abandoned military installation taken over by squatters in 1971, just barely tolerated now as a social experiment in conflict with the police and the conservative citizenry. Through the front gate, he walks the unstreetlighted, frozen, rutted mud of the path to Pusher Street, sparsely populated this freezing night, toward the JazzKlub. The shutters are open at the entrance, and he steps in.

The girl at the door says, "Nothing really happening yet."

"If I can just get a beer while I wait."

"Just holler into the kitchen for the bartender."

Bluett pays his forty-*kroner* entry and holds out his hand for her to scribble on it with a marker so he can return to the club if he steps out for a joint, but she says, "Forgot the marker today. I'll remember you. I know your face. I've seen you before."

"Did I behave in an orderly manner?"

"I don't remember what you did, but I don't have bad memories of you."

The bartender, a dark-haired man who speaks Danish with a Spanish accent, is already at the bar. He recognizes Bluett from previous visits. It's nice to be recognized. Bluett passes him a twenty-*kroner* coin for a bottle of red-label beer. The first patron in the place, he has his pick of tables, each different, some metal, some wood. He picks one that has an overview of the whole club and all of its black walls and pipes. There are also long benches against the long back wall of the little room, beneath a row of oil paintings of jazz artists, only one of whom he recognizes: the great tenor sax player Dexter Gordon, wearing a long coat on his tall frame, a leopard-skin hat perched on his head.

Over the sound system come Dizzy Gillespie and Charlie Parker blowing "Night in Tunisia," written by Diz in 1942. He remembers one day the previous July during the Jazz Festival, sitting in the sun all day drinking golden pints of draft on the canal at Gammel Strand, listening to the Esben Malø Quartet, young musicians—trumpet, tenor, contrabass, el guitar—play cool jazz in the hot afternoon while kayaks and yachts with half-naked people sunning on the foredecks and flat canal boats of waving tourists floated past—right across from Thorvaldsens Museum, yellow sun high in the arch of the blue sky, points of light glittering on the green tower of the parliament and the black tile roofs of the pastel-colored canal houses—and the red-headed young trumpeter blew an approximation of Cannonball Adderley's version of "Autumn Leaves," a cool subject for a hot day, and the breeze ruffled the edges of the broad white umbrellas over their stage area. He had watched a two-man kayak lance past in the water, the back space empty, while the sunlight tingled his flesh.

Life is gorgeous sometimes.

Bluett had asked the cool young quartet if they would play "Night in Tunisia," but the trumpeter had confided he was too hungover to take on that number. Now it's playing on the JazzKlub's sound system, and those two simple disparate experiences make him feel some manner of continuity.

He wonders that he has been drinking all day and is not getting drunk. Unless he's in that dangerous sort of drunkenness where he's so drunk that he doesn't think he's drunk.

The singer and her guitarist, Kelley and Tony, are setting up on the stage now, and people are drifting in. Kelley and Tony are joined by a visiting alto sax man from Russia, a Danish guy with an electric guitar, a bass man, a drummer. The music is mellow. It seems to be one of those days when no matter how much Bluett drinks, it just keeps him on Mellow Street. Kelley is singing "What Is This Thing Called Love?," her voice cool and clear, and the Russian laces around her words with alto riffs, and the guitar notes glide so cool and so electric into the dim smoky light of the club.

A dog is wandering around among the tables, one of the most beautiful dogs Bluett has ever seen, a mix of golden and collie and husky with a beautiful white coat, immaculately brushed. He makes welcoming lip noises to attract the dog, and it noses over, makes a polite perfunctory greeting, allows Bluett to scratch its neck for a minute then wanders off, and Kelley is singing bossa nova in Portuguese, and through some incalculable series of maneuvers, somehow Bluett finds himself speaking with the owner of the dog who is every bit as gorgeous as her dog—and sweet and friendly and nicely shaped. Her name is Lucia. Maybe she will be the light of Bluett's life.

He wonders if Lucia will decide she likes him. The woman always decides whether it is a possibility. Otherwise it's rape. Tell you their decision with a smile—of rue or complicity or surrender. Rue means you get nada, with complicity you're in for a good time, but with surrender you're just in for it. He is looking at Lucia, and she smiles at him—what kind of smile? he wonders, but doesn't really care; it is just so goddamn nice to be smiled at by a sweet woman. She touches his arm and asks if he would like to share a joint with her in the kitchen.

Then they are in the kitchen, and she is sitting on the deep kitchen sideboard with her legs stretched out, and her toenails are polished plum blue, and he tokes the joint and studies her clean, beautiful feet. He wants to touch and to kiss them. Tentatively, he lays a fingertip on Lucia's toes, and she does not protest. In fact, she touches his arm again and asks if he is married.

"I haven't had sex in a year," she says.

Out in the club Kelley is singing "How About You?" and then "Lovers and Friends." He is wondering how old Lucia is, notices that her face is not exactly beautiful, as he had thought, but more attractive in an unusual way. She has an agreeable voice—a voice Bluett could definitely fall for. He keeps stealing glances at her face to determine what precisely constitutes its unusualness. By now his fingers are massaging her feet, and she is leaning back on her elbows and telling Bluett about her work as a cemetery tour guide.

Bluett is confused. He thinks that he might have misheard, due to the tokes. He says, "What, like, you are some kind of real estate purveyor for people who want to be buried?"

She laughs. She has a nice laugh. He could definitely fall for that laugh but is still confused at this business about a cemetery tour guide. From a dainty pink backpack, she removes a card that she extends to him. It shows the name of a tour guide bureau specializing in cemeteries and cemetery sculpture. She says that she shows groups around on walking tours of various cemeteries, gives talks on who is buried where. "You know," she says. "The graves of the famous."

She lights another joint and passes it, and he tokes and finds himself staring into the shadows of the corner. Time has that strange quality dope sometimes gives it. Then Getz is on the sound system, blowing Billy Strayhorn's "Blood Count," and Lucia and Bluett go back into the heart of the club. The lights are even dimmer than before, and most of the guests are gone, and Bluett wonders what was in that dope and can't quite recall how many joints they smoked.

The bartender with the Spanish accent produces a soprano sax from beneath the bar and starts blowing to a guitar backup. The soprano notes are like a fine fine grade of sturdy sculpted tin in the dim light. Lucia sits on a bench and pats the space beside her for him to sit, which he does and then he hears himself asking, "Can I call you?"

To which she replies. "As long as you realize it will never be more than friendship."

Bluett wonders how in the world he managed to fuck *that* up. He says, "Well, what's wrong with friendship?" And then they are at the bar, and Bluett looks at his watch. Somehow the long day and night have melted into quarter to two in the A.M. Lucia is talking to the owner, and now Bluett is no longer getting drunk. He *is* drunk. Maybe *that* was how he fucked it up. He sees two bartenders blowing two sopranos. At first it's, like, double your pleasure. But then it's, like, time to go home.

The front doors are locked so he threads through the back rooms and hallways until he discovers an unlocked door and steps out into the dark, freezing morning. He walks the dirt street toward the Free State exit and sees the familiar raw wood sign over it into which is carved, on this side, YOU ARE NOW ENTERING THE EUROPEAN UNION. He steps through the gate, under the sign, and is out on the street just in time to flag a Mercedes taxi.

As the cab rolls over Knippels Bridge, black water gleaming on either side, the green copper towers of Copenhagen up ahead cloaked in darkness, he says to the Iranian driver, "All in all, as Ivan Denisovich put it in nineteen sixty-two, it has been a good day."

The driver chuckles, and Bluett knows he has no idea what Bluett is talking about.

5. Aura

Sunday. Already light when he wakes so he knows it is at least nine thirty or ten, reaches for his watch: 10:20. In the kitchen he spoons coffee into the electric maker for a whole pot and waits, leaden-eyed, until it drips its last into the glass pot, pours a mug of black and wanders into the living room. He sees the CD jacket of Miles Davis's *Aura* and remembers how he had been waylaid the previous day, or was it the day before that, from listening all the way through.

Slowly the scraps of memory of Saturday reassemble in his mind: walking through the Botanical Garden, the Booktrader, Café Halfway... *Halfway through my life I found myself on a dark path...*

Unspecified sandwiches, more walking, lamb curry, the JazzKlub, the drinks, the dope... Lucia. His brain is post-dope hazy but not disagreeably so.

He pours coffee down his neck, fumbles through his pockets for the card she gave him, finds it, sees and remembers that she is a cemetery guide, thinks you couldn't ever make this shit up. He tears up the card and drops it in the garbage along with the wet coffee grounds.

Another mug and he puts on *Aura*, thinking, the day yesterday was a mere, albeit a pleasant, interruption. Lucia's aura did not admit you. You did not have the chemistry that perked her percolator. What is chemistry anyway? Mystery. But undeniable.

Something makes him think of a woman named Johanna who wanted him to spank her, and he did it, but she said, *Not that way!* And taught him how she wanted to be spanked, starting with a gentle caress and building up... He felt like a dunce for not knowing that. But now he knows how, should he be called upon to administer what the Danes call an "end-full." So many things a man is called upon to know.

In his one good armchair he sits with the hot mug balanced on his knee and listens, eyes closed, to Miles, playing the symphony Palle Mikkelborg wrote for him two years before Miles died, six years earlier. He hears John

McLaughlin's guitar opening the piece, and Miles's unmistakable trumpet, a tom-tom. He remembers the first time he heard this CD was in the Fiver (Femmeren) on Classensgade. A tall young guy next to him at the bar asked the bartender to play the CD and told Bluett that Miles hadn't worn his headphones when he played trumpet over McLaughlin's guitar and all the other musicians. At first Bluett thought he was saying it had been careless of Miles, but then he saw the young guy could see that thought on his face and the guy quickly added, "That was part of his process on that recording. I can understand that, what he got from using that technique."

Afterward the young man left, and Bluett asked the bartender to play *Aura* once again, and the bartender said, "You know who that guy was? It was Halfdan E. He's a composer. He composed the music on the two Dan Turèll CDs. Lots else, too."

Funny, he thinks, *how in Copenhagen everybody mixes. No one is too famous to hang around with whomever.*

Now Bluett can't hear this music without thinking about that, about how ingenious it was of Miles, how that information from Halfdan E enabled him to understand this music much more deeply. And he thinks about what Palle Mikkelborg writes inside the CD case: "I still thank my guardian angel for giving me the marvelous gift of meeting and working with this true master who, before we ever met, had already changed my life."

Bluett thinks about that statement, thinks that this music in some way has changed him as well, and he doesn't know how, but he knows that it is so. The music swells within him, and a name enters his head. Liselotte. They were lovers years earlier when they both were married to other people. She was young and beautiful and he was young and naïve and both were locked in disagreeable marriages with kids too young to leave. He heard recently that she had divorced again a while back. He hasn't seen her for a dozen years, but she once told him, *Call anytime, Blue, I'm always home for you.* He looks for his phone book, finds it under a heap of papers on his desk, and is punching in the numbers, listening to the ring as he watches the now yellow sunlight across the lake and hears Miles blowing the "Yellow" cut.

"Hej! Det er Liselotte!"

So cheerful. "I didn't wake you?" He remembers she is an early riser, remembers that she too liked to make love in the morning.

"Hej, Blue!"

"Wow, you have a great memory for voices!"

"I always remember your voice."

"Listen," he says. "I wanted to call you, tell you that I got divorced."

"Velcome to the club," she says. She has been divorced two times, and they talk about the experience—how it is not fun, how you always wonder if you really did enough, tried enough, and of course no one ever does, but it also takes give from the other side, but sometimes you also wonder if maybe the problem is that you gave *too* much, that you should have put your foot down instead of trying to understand, and who ever knows really, maybe in fact marriage is an outmoded institution, maybe we are evolving toward some other form of society, but sometimes it is hard to see any way around the fact that the basic unit would always be one man and one woman with children, but of course it is entirely possible to love many persons at one and the same time, and who is to say what is right, and in truth sometimes there comes a time when you know deep down in your heart that a marriage is over, done, dead, harmful, nothing left but two people full of contempt for one another and what is left to do then but get out and try to do it as gently and understandingly as possible even though probably no one ever really manages to be gentle or understanding and probably no divorce is reasonable or civilized despite your best intentions because the emotions involved are not civilized emotions, there is always rage and sorrow and deep pain and there is a time when more than anything you need your friends, it is not fun, maybe at first you feel good to be alone but after a while, well, who knows? Maybe it will be different for you so why should I try to discourage you and it is true that it is beautiful to be master or mistress of your own time, your own life, your own apartment, but one thing you surely do need is friends and please know that if you need someone to talk to, and I don't care what time of day it is, I am here for you, just call, just come and knock on my door, Blue, I'm here.

"That means a lot to me," he says. "Friends are important."

"Do you have friends?"

"A few."

"Well, I hope you will be counting me as one."

"That means a lot to me."

"How is it going for you in this time?"

"Actually I feel pretty good. It was the right thing. I can feel that."

"Then you are lucky. You have done the right thing. It is not good to be together with someone you cannot love or speak with."

"What I want now is a single life. I want never to get myself into a tangled-up situation like that again."

"Love is never simple."

"I don't want love. Not like that. I don't know what love is. If love turns into what my marriage turned into, I don't want it. I want friends. I want lots of friends. I want to feel alive and open for a change. I've had my kids. What else is marriage for but to have kids? And I've had my kids, I have them. Now I want a different life for myself. I want to be free to enjoy life."

"The good life," she says. "I hope you can be able to find it."

He doesn't know what to say to that, so he says "Well, I do want a lover, someone to love," and there is a silence until she says, "I have been missing to hear your voice."

"I've thought about you," he says.

"Have you?"

Now he is busy. He vacuums the beige carpet in the living room, the gray one in the bedroom, fits on the long-snouted attachment and gets the dust behind the radiators, the wispy spidery gatherings up in the corners of the ceiling.

He fills a bucket with hot water and Ajax liquid and sponges off the white woodwork, the bathroom sink, kitchen sink, makes the chrome faucets gleam. He scours the tub and shower walls, scrubs out the toilet bowl, gets down on hands and knees and washes the kitchen and bathroom floors with a soapy rag, outside the commode.

Then he gathers up old magazines and newspapers, junk mail, brochures from tabletops and window ledges. He dusts, shakes the cloth out the window, gives it another once-over, flushes the dirty bucket water down the toilet to a background of Coltrane's "Favorite Things," showers and washes his hair.

He shaves, slowly lathers up and scrapes the blade across his jowls, brushes his teeth, gargles, clips his nose hair with mustache scissors, trims his 'stache, trying to clip most of the gray and leave the red, brown, and black hairs. He picks out his newest Calvin Klein underwear, a clean blue shirt, his favorite tie and pullover, clean pressed Levis. He polishes his shoes and goes out to stock up for the evening.

At the Irma supermarket he loads a basket with candles, Crémant, Cabernet, Asian snacks, chips, a couple of nice-looking slabs of entrecôte, onions, lettuce hearts and cherry tomatoes, a beautiful wedge of Gorgonzola at the perfect moment of its existence, a fresh-baked baguette. He joins the line at the checkout counter behind an elderly man, who doesn't have a basket or a cart, seems to have no wares, only a walker. A hearing aid is visible among the sparse white hairs on his round head.

When his turn comes, he says, "I don't know if I should be here."

The girl at the register blinks. "Did you want to buy anything?" she asks.

In mild, apologetic confusion, the man says, "I think I was supposed to have a blood test." He smiles self-deprecatingly and turns around, looks into Bluett's eyes, then turns back toward the exit door. "Excuse me," he mutters. "Excuse me. So sorry."

One by one, Bluett lays the items in his basket on the counter, meets the young girl's helpless eyes with an equally helpless expression in his.

"Maybe you should call the authorities," he suggests quietly.

"You think so? The emergency number?"

"Yes," he says, but she rings up his wares before calling, and when Bluett walks through the automatic doors of the supermarket, passes a cluster of parked bicycles, the old man is nowhere in sight. He looks up and down the street, watches a red-nosed, sniffling woman clatter her bike over the cobblestones, swing up onto the saddle.

The sunlight gleams across the frozen lake now and church bells boom the hour as he climbs the wooden staircase to his apartment, thinking about the old man, thinking he should have stayed with him. Would have been about the age of Bluett's father. Had he lived. Had he not had his heart attack twenty-five years earlier. Bluett was eighteen. In 1972. *Dad was fifty-five. No age.*

After dinner, he plays *Aura* for Liselotte as they sip their cognac by candle flame.

"I am loving your apartment," she says.

"It was the first one I looked at. I fell in love with the view but I figured, you can't buy the first apartment you look at. So I looked at ten others, each one more depressing than the other, and came back for this. Almost didn't get it, had someone bidding against me. Some rich dad wanted to buy it for his daughter who was in college. Even sent me a threatening letter. Nasty piece of work. The apartment is nothing special, but I need this view. It told me I could be happy here."

"I could be happy here, too," she says, and there is an awkward moment. "I mean . . ." She laughs, and it passes, her pretty face older now than when he last saw her. Her neck. He feels shallow for noticing this, but he notices. Still, she looks good, trim and shapely with delicate pretty hands. He loves her hands, and sparkling pale brown eyes the color of a shot of Wild Turkey bourbon held to the light, he thinks. Hundred proof. Her pretty mouth. A brown-eyed blonde. Sweet woman.

"I like your aura," he says, making a private joke about the title of the music, but she gets it. She puts her hand on his arm. They sit side by side on the sofa.

"This music is so beautiful," she says. "So powerful."

He kisses her, and they put down their glasses, and it all comes back to him, how passionate she was, how they fit together, how much fun she was in bed, the games they played. Eccentric ideas excite her, and her excitement excites him.

His bed is uncomfortably narrow for the two of them so they spread a blanket on the floor, and afterward, he lies on his back, staring up through slitted eyes at the ceiling, drifting away.

She says, "I hope the neighbors couldn't hear. Was I too loud?"

"Let them eat their hearts out."

She says, "Where did you learn that? What you did with my hair?"

He smiles at her, takes her light hair in his fingers. It occurs to him she must color it. He tugs a little.

"Ow," she says.

"Oh, sorry."

She smiles. "Don't be." And he rolls toward her again. She whispers something, and he is on her, hears her voice in his ear calling out word-lessly—what he has missed these months alone, what he missed all the last barren years with his ex, what he couldn't get with Benthe because it was too much of a sport with her.

By three, he is exhausted and she sleeps on her side beneath the feather blanket he has draped across her. She snores gently, a light femi-nine snore. She is so feminine. He feels lucky to be with her. He pours a vodka and puts on *Aura* again, very low, and sits by the window watch-ing the lake.

She is gone when he wakes and someone is hammering at the door. He is in his bed, naked. He grabs a robe, sees a note on the table—*Dear you, I have to leave for work. Call me tonight? Me.*

The hammering at the door continues.

"All right, all right," he shouts and opens the door.

Sam Finglas stands there with a pitcher of red stuff. "Bloody bloody," he says. "Just the ticket for a man who drank and fucked too much last night. Got yourself a moaner, ey, boyo?"

"Christ," he says. "It's fucking Monday morning! Maybe you're inde-pendently wealthy, but *I've* got to work, Sam."

"Best time to do something beautiful is when you're supposed to be doing something else."

They sit at his oak table with the pitcher. Bluett figures it for madness, but it's already ten, and the night has left him with a laid-back hang-over—another laid-back hangover. He puts on music. This cold sunny day he goes for Dire Straits, Mark Knopfler singing about his honey of a conductress on the number 18, and they sip bloody Marys watching the lake to a background of Knopfler's elegant guitar.

Finglas lights a King, inhales as if the smoke is air and he's dying for breath.

"Don't get a hernia, Sam."

"Funny." He raises his glass, drinks. "So, how was your night?"

"Pretty good."

"Got lucky, huh? Her moans rattled my windowpanes."

"Don't talk to me about luck. I *saw* your Russki girlfriend."

Finglas glances with startled eyes. "*Where? When?*"

"Over on Nyhavn. Just glimpsed her through the crowd, the two of you, walking together." He thinks of the Satin Room, wants to ask. "She's a knockout."

Finglas looks thoughtful, like he's trying to remember something.

"Still happy with her?" Bluett asks.

He just shakes his head in slow wonderment and appreciation.

Knopfler is singing about French kisses in the dark, and Bluett smacks his lips over the tang of vodka and Tabasco on his tongue.

"Listen, Blue, mind if I put something in your storage room, a box?"

"You run out of space?"

"Some stuff I, uh, wouldn't want my family to see. If anything happened to me I mean."

"Always wear clean underwear 'case you get run down. 'Course, then you probably crap yourself anyway."

"So, is it okay?"

Bluett thinks about some stuff he has, couple of magazines, some letters, a video, he wouldn't care to have his daughter see. He has been thinking of burning them, but hasn't got round to it. "'Course. Feel free. It's not locked. I ought to store a box with you."

Finglas chuckles. "Porn stock, eh? Never been a man alone doesn't have one. Best medicine. Stick of weed and a hot film. Aside from the real thing. Ooo." He shifts tenderly in his chair. "I am tapped out. My plums have turned to prunes."

"Alchemy, eh? She's that good?"

"Better."

"The lock on my storage room in the basement won't lock," Bluett says. "So put anything in there you want. Best not put any black-market cash, though."

"I wish," Sam says.

58

The bloodies are doing their job on Bluett. Now Knopfler sings about sweet surrender, and Bluett catches himself studying the quality of the light, the grace of the dozen skaters out on the lake, feels a smile on his numb lips as his eyes take in the patches of light on the ice. What *is* light? he thinks, and the question amuses him. He glances at Finglas, sees a shadow in his eyes. "Anything wrong, Sam?"

He shrugs. "The ex. Phone call this morning."

"Give you a hard time?"

"As only *she* can."

Knopfler is proposing to a waitress in the wild West End, and Bluett does not want to think gloomy thoughts about ex-wives. "What is this world?" he recites. "What asketh man to have? Now with his love, now in his cold grave," pronouncing "have" and "grave" as two syllables, Middle English style.

"Amen. How's business?"

"Fair. Want company for dinner tonight?"

"Got an appointment."

"You dog." He remembers Liselotte. "Actually I might have an appointment myself."

Sam sits back in his chair, one arm draped behind him, the other holding his bloody Mary on his knee, as he stares at the tall bookcase that fills the end wall of the apartment. "Jesus," he murmurs. "All those books. I used to read, you know." He looks at Bluett. "Can't for the life of me remember why."

Bluett sniggers, realizes it is not meant as a joke.

"It used to seem so . . . goddamn important, like something important happening with every book I put into me. Goddamned if I know what. Nah. It's the senses that occupy me now." He looks at Bluett again, and his eyes glitter, the tips of his thumb and two fingers moving gently together. "You know. To *be*."

"Or not to be," sings Bluett. "That's the question but not for me . . ." Old Danish razzmatazz. Reasonably sloshed himself, he watches Sam's fingers, the fine contact between them, mesmerized by the quality of his voice, his words, remembering Liselotte's body in the dark on the floor, the light of stars and moon through the window illuminating her pale flesh. "Yeah," he breathes. "Sacrament of the senses. *Ite missa est.* The Mass is over. All for it. Light a candle to their lovelies."

Bluett thinks once again of telling him about Benthe, the ménage à trois, but realizes once again that he does not want to tell about that. It's done. *Ite missa est.*

When the pitcher is empty, Finglas takes his leave with it. Bluett still has half a glass of bloody, which he freshens from his own stock. He sits by the window in the silence, tired of music, thinking of Liselotte's breasts, how perfectly they curved against her ribs, and how they felt against his palms, how her lips parted and teeth glinted when he touched the nipples, how soft her skin was against his cheek, her thigh, the blonde nest, shot through with gray. *To be.*

At four thirty, he takes a chance and tries her number, and she gets it on the first ring, her voice full of light, like a bird, like an angel. "I left the office early today," she explains, "hoping you would call. Couldn't wait."

6. Noise Rock: Arab on Radar

Their dinner that evening is cheese and baguettes and radishes with a bottle of Cab, a second in waiting. Bluett has power-napped the bloodies off and showered and feels mellow by the candlelight, puts on a CD his daughter forgot when she visited him the previous week. A group called Arab on Radar that she said was "Noise Rock." Eric Paul and Andrea Fiset singing "Rough Day at the Orifice." Bluett wonders what he thinks about his daughter listening to such stuff, then remembers that it was she who turned him on to Prince's "Sexy M.F.," which utterly repulsed him at first, until he opened to it and realized, without ever knowing it, that that's just what a man thinks. As James Joyce taught him to listen to his thoughts, Prince did, too. Apparently a process that never is quite done.

Bluett breaks a raw egg yolk over his Gorgonzola and half-listens to Liselotte's chatter. He feels fresh, randy for a long night. He's been hungry too long. *Way of life*, he thinks. *Feast or famine.* You want it so bad or you wonder what the hell it's for, all the clawing in the dark.

She says, "You should have some plants here. Some flowers."

He glances at the five window ledges, white-lacquered wood, bare but for a hand-painted vase, a piece of crystal. "Plants die," he says. "Flowers wither. They're lost on me. But if you like 'em . . ."

He changes the CD to Billie Holiday's *Silver Collection*, Ben Webster on tenor, and he takes Liselotte's fine little sculpted hand and leads her out onto the carpet. She watches him with happy submissive eyes, something he loves in her. *That gaze goes straight to my baguette.*

"I wished on the moon," he whisper-sings in her ear as they dance slow, close, her leg between his, his between hers. What life is for. He nuzzles her neck, unbuttons her blouse, and it is as he remembers, better.

They dance naked by candlelight, Carole King singing now, and Blue sings along in Liselotte's ear, hears his own voice, high but sounding in harmony, singing about unspoken words saying you're the only one, and they lie down on the carpet, and she whispers, "You've got to buy a bigger bed," and he says, "I love the floor," hearing the faint slur in his words as he glides into a moment so huge he forgets it will ever end.

All things are temporal. This too shall pass, he thinks as he sits over his translation in the gray Tuesday light, waiting for the codeine tablets to do their thing and fix up his head so he can catch up on the five pages of translation he hadn't done the previous day.

Liselotte has a real job with a boss she has to bring coffee to and write letters for and run and hop for, so he cannot phone her for—he checks his watch—seven hours. He wants more of the same. That was what she had said to him the previous night. After he went down on her, and she went down on him, and he pulled her hair and squeezed her butt till she squeaked, she whispered, "I want more of the same."

Like Sam said. To be. What life is for, he thinks with his red Gyldendal Danish-English, English-Danish dictionaries spread out on the desk before him, coffee, juice, pills. He pops a lump of sugar from the bowl, crunches it between his teeth, sips black coffee through the crystals, a trick he learned from a Norwegian girl. Used to drive his wife crazy. *Only peasants do that!*

As the sugar shoots to his brain, he thinks of other sweet games to play with her, wonders why he didn't think of her before, thinks of sweet what's-her-name that he met in Nyhavn, what *was* her name? Birgitte! Birgitte Svane. Who kissed so nice and sucked his tongue. Give her a call. He and Liselotte talked in the middle of it all about another woman. Were you ever with another woman? Would you?

She thought for a moment, said, "She would have to be very special."

And he thought about Benthe and Dorte and what they had done up in the cottage in Halvstrand, and he said to Liselotte, "It's only a fantasy. Best keep it that way. That way we can have fun with it."

Now he gets up from his desk, walks to the kitchen, douses his face with water from the faucet, paces the length of the apartment's front wall, five double windows over the lake.

He has only done three pages today so far. He reminds himself that he is seven pages behind, that he has to do five pages a day to stay here in this apartment. He owns the apartment, but the bank owns him. If he loses the apartment he can survive, but life will not be good, there will be pressure, no surplus, no vodka ad libitum, like that streak of bad luck a few years back when the only drink he could afford was cheap Danish vermouth. Bad scene. Vermouth on the rocks your only solace. Get you high, but with an aftertaste. And no room to maneuver. *Why do you drink so much? Just to numb that tip of consciousness that can't forget. Forget what? Who knows? The reaper maybe.*

He thinks again of Liselotte's breasts, her smiling teeth in the candlelight. *More of the same, please.* Then he goes to the kitchen again and douses his face, his wrists, drinks a glass of club soda straight down, pees and gets back to his desk. She will leave the office at five thirty, get home by six. He sets his wrist alarm for six P.M., the earliest time that he can phone her. Then he puts his mind to the remainder of the instructions for use for the turnkey summer-house rentals.

The weeks are charmed. More of the same, again and again. One week, two weeks, into a third, and a fourth, they are together nearly every evening, every night, alternating between his place and hers.

They listen to jazz at the White Lamb, jazz on CD and tape cassette at Femmeren on Classensgade, to all the Central European minstrels along Nyhavn, hunched in their overcoats. They go to museums, to Glyptoteket and look at the sculpture of the Water Mother, white and naked and graceful in the center of the fountain pond, a dozen marble babies crawling up from the water for her breasts, one seated in the crook of her upturned arm, all surrounded by palm trees beneath the domed glass. They stroll through the gallery of Roman busts, and Bluett looks at face after face, two-thousand-year-old expressions no different than the faces you see now, around you every day, personalities caught in stone. He studies a five-thousand-year-old Mesopotamian lion relief cut in stone, fading, almost completely faded, indistinct. He can just glimpse the last vague lines of it—an ancient thing on the edge of extinction. Like Rilke's poem to his father's photograph: *Oh, slowly fading portrait in my more slowly fading hand.*

Good-bye, lion. Good-bye.

They take long walks and look at the street sculpture, the underwater statues of the merman and his sons beneath the canal reaching up to the surface, imploring the human woman who has left them to return, naked Diana on a horse at Trondhjemsplads (outside the Danish Medical Association, from which he gets a lot of translation business), the massive statues representing the Nile and Tiber rivers, depicted as reclining figures in green bronze flanking the south ramp of Queen Louise's Bridge, the bronze reclining nude on the grass at Gronningen, so sensual she excites them both.

For further inspiration, they visit the Museum Erotica on Købmagergade, where, as they stand looking at a photograph of the longest recorded human penis in history, thirty-two centimeters slack, she whispers in his ear, "I want my mouth full of your prick."

He whispers, "And I want to eat your cunt."

They take a walk down Istedgade and browse through the sex shops at toys and magazines. At Playtime they rent a couple of adult videos to do instant replay on scenes they want to try. At the S and M shop on Studiestræde, they buy a toy that he uses on her, and then she uses on him, and as they lie there afterward, she plays with the hair on his chest and asks if he has ever spanked a woman.

He sips the Alsatian champagne they bought at Irma's. They smile at each other, discussing it delicately, playing with the thought, while he secretly thanks the woman who taught him how to do it.

"Where?" he asks. "Here?" Touching her bottom gently with his palm. She nods, smiling. "Yeah!" she whispers.

Then they talk about another woman again, searching through the names of women they both know to see if there is one they both would like, discussing them, their bodies, their faces, their manner, considering different games they could play with them, all the while Bluett realizing it is only a fantasy, only a thought to excite them. He opens another bottle of champagne.

It makes him begin to ask himself again about what love is. Can it be something as simple as this? To share life like this? Just unwrap, unwire, uncork the champagne and enjoy one another, and nothing else is required? Let there be spaces in your togetherness. He remembers something he read about the true religion of our time, that it is not a religion of death and sacrifice, but one of pleasure and joy and human communion and comingling. Yet he is skeptical, reminds himself of the importance of maintaining a healthy skepticism of human motives, one's own and others'.

He phones his oldest sister Noreen, in New Haven, who has lived apart from her husband for the past several years. "I could never trust him again," she says. "He lied to me too many times."

"Is it so bad?" Bluett asks. "That a man has those desires, those needs?"

"I have no problem with that," Noreen says. "But I can not abide lying."

"Would you have tolerated it if he had been honest and told you about it?"

"Then we would have dealt with it."

In the afternoons when his pages are done, he walks through the city, thinking. Noreen is probably the person in the world that he is closest to now, after his children. Her husband, she learned one day, had had a mistress for nearly ten years. He wept and ended it when Noreen found out and he vowed to be faithful, and five years later she found out there had been a new one almost immediately after the split with the first one. He could not explain himself. She could not tolerate the lies. So now they live apart, but still are married and devoted to one another.

Bluett cannot come to terms with it. The problem feels foreign to him.

He circles the lake, wind whistling across, sliding icily over his face. Sometimes it moans in the courtyard behind the house, and he lies in bed listening to it, staring up at the white ceiling, wondering where he is. It is late afternoon. A lone couple walks across the blue ice, same blue color as the dusky sky, and just three kids left on skates, silhouettes gliding from sight.

There is a voice behind him, a woman's, oddly pitched. A girl walks past, alone, reading aloud from a sheet of paper: "My parents don't understand the situation and I am losing my mind . . ." Bluett slows his pace to fall behind, and her voice trails off. He feels guilty that he could not offer her help.

He crosses over from the lakes to the other side of Nørreport, strolls down Købmagergade, passes the jewelry store where he bought the rings for his wedding twenty-one years earlier.

My heart is broken, he thinks, *that my marriage has failed. Where is my wife, my only wife whom I can no longer bear to be in the same room with, nor she with me?*

He considers again about the religion of pleasure, thinks, *I'm not sure we're made for pleasure. We're turned into orgasm dogs, pawing the orgasm button till we perish from neglect of our other needs. We are not meant to be happy. Guilt and sorrow is our natural lot.*

A young man passes him on the street, a dark, pallid, pimply youth with hollow purple-ringed eyes, a head too big for his body, and a haunted look on his features. *Why should that boy be so lost and miserable? My sorrow is as nothing beside his.*

Now he sees a group of children wearing animal masks and carrying clubs, another kid dressed like a gypsy, and after a moment of disoriented horror, he realizes it is Fastelavn, the old pagan feast that Lent replaced. In olden days, the Danes sealed a black cat in a barrel, strung it up, and beat the barrel with clubs until it broke open and the cat, driven mad, escaped. Nowadays they use an empty barrel, paste a picture of a cat on it, and fill it with goodies. It makes him wonder about the Danes, but of course he knows you could find something as strange or stranger anywhere, and as he passes a kiosk, he glances at the newspaper headline display that says GENOME WARFARE WEAPONS AIMED TO SELECT RACIAL TRAITS, and he decides to stop for a cup of coffee at the Clapboard Café on the Coal Square.

A familiar face is leaving the café, a woman. She smiles, nods. One of his neighbors. He remembers hearing her cry out in passion one night a few weeks earlier, long wracking cries that had him sit up in bed, made him feel the gleam of his own eyes, confirming something there in the lonely night, holding promise.

As he drinks his coffee, he watches a woman at a table by the window eating a salad with bread and club soda. She eats slowly, with obvious pleasure; her face is natural, attractive in its plainness, and she looks so happy and lovely he wishes he could be her.

When he gets home, his son, Timothy, is waiting for him at the door, and Bluett's heart lifts.

"Eh, Daddio!" Tim says and swings one arm around his father.

"Timmy, boy!"

The boy now stands half a head taller than Bluett, who continues to feel startled at his transformation from child to man. The boy's life is recorded in Bluett's brain in a series of snapshots. Mental photo album. Bluett can sit in his armchair in the dark and close his eyes and leaf through the pages and see Tim at six months, gnawing with relish at a hunk of cucumber, his face bright with the pleasure of being alive; can see Tim running gleefully toward him down the driveway as Bluett returned at evening from the office job he had for a time; can remember carrying him upstairs to lay him in his cradle to sleep. *This is a memory to cherish when old/Climbing upstairs with a bundle of gold.* From his earliest years, the boy had combined a mix of quick wit and compassionate heart that was compensation to Bluett for every bad moment of his life, though it pained him as nothing else could that his son's wounds over the divorce had not yet healed.

Tim's hair is cut very short, a translucent dark fuzz against his skull. Opposite of Bluett's own hair-revolution when he was a kid in the seventies. But how could he complain about that? *Hey, Tim, don't you think it's about time to stop getting so many haircuts?*

Inside the apartment he ushers the boy into the living room. "What can I get you, son? Beer? Something stronger?"

"Ah . . . just a Coke, thanks, Dad. I can't stay long. Got a lot of reading to do."

Bluett knows he has to watch himself, not to scare the boy off, not to say anything that might cause him to disappear deep into his anger, out of reach. He recognizes that the anger over the divorce is combined with the natural resentment a twenty-one-year-old feels for his father, recognizes that Timothy's way of expressing this is a kind of vague cool disdain that he keeps ready to use as necessary and that his own desire to force through that shield will help nothing. He has to relax with it. It only comes in spurts, on occasion; otherwise his son is warm and full of humor. He just never expected anything to come between them. The two of them had always been so close, had spent so much time together. He knows he has made mistakes, said awkward, regrettable things, but still they had shared such a good life together that he never expected such a wedge could appear between them. He remembers a period when Tim was thirteen or so when if they walked the street together the boy would lay his palm on Bluett's shoulder, walking a little bit behind—allowing his father to lead him. He wonders if that same closeness will reappear in time, wonders if children and parents simply part ways at some point and perhaps this is that point for Timothy. There is a Danish saying, "Once they let go of your hand, they never take it again," which terrifies Bluett. But he will not let the boy go. Never. He will nurture the memories of their closeness, will nurture the memory of the picture Timothy had drawn for him once when he came home from a business trip: a boy standing on the deck of a boat smiling, his arms open in greeting over the caption WELCOME HOME, CAPTAIN DAD! And the time that Bluett had some success with a literary translation he had done and was the subject of an article in the newspaper, and Timothy had looked into his eyes and said with emotion, "I am so proud of you, Dad."

"And I'm proud of you, Tim. I am so proud of you."

Bluett sips a beer while his son drinks the Coke and the afternoon sun disappears into the ice on the lake.

"How's your girl, Tim? Kristine, right?"

"Yeah, right. She's fine."

Bluett has not been allowed to meet her yet, although she and Tim have been together for almost a year. Bluett's daughter has met her, told him a little. She is the daughter of a surgeon, very mild and intelligent.

"How's school?"

The boy smirks slightly, shrugs. "Boring."

Bluett chuckles. "I remember I said that once to someone, a colleague, and he said, 'Boring is not a problem. Boring one can always cope with.'"

Tim's eyes flash. "It's still boring, Dad!"

"Well, you'll be finished soon, then you can take a break, travel some."

"Yeah. *If* I finish."

Weapon. Bad tact. Avoid this. Yet he finds himself playing right into it. "You'll destroy your best chances if you quit now."

"I'm not talking about quitting. I'm just thinking about taking a year off."

"You take a year off, you may never get back to it. Then you'll be stuck. I know what I'm talking about. I took a leave of absence at the beginning of my university studies when I came to Denmark, and it took me three years to get back into it. I couldn't finish until I got here, and it ruined my chances for an academic career."

"Who wants an academic career?"

"You might. You can't know yet for sure. Don't cut yourself off. Don't shut the door on yourself." Bluett hears what he is saying, hears cliché after cliché, knows that he is saying what he wishes his own father had said to him all those years before instead of giving him permission to do as he pleased, make his own mistakes, his father who was too lost in *his* and then died. Yet at the same time he senses that nothing can be accomplished with this conversation. Perhaps it is enough just to register his resistance. Change the subject.

"You going away for winter recess, Tim? Do some skiing maybe?"

"Who has money for that?"

The silence extends as Bluett thinks about this, thinks he recognizes where the conversation is headed, wonders if he has set himself up for it, if the whole purpose of the visit was a touch, and why should it be otherwise? He doesn't mind, he doesn't mind giving the boy money; he just hates the thought that it might have been the whole purpose of the visit, hates his own suspicion that it might have been engineered by smirks and bitter comments and wonders if it is his own fault that it happens this way. Does he keep too tight a hand on his wallet? Does he use money as bait to draw the kids to him? And what kind of person is he to expect it to be otherwise, to crave this level of devotion?

For a moment he considers making the boy bite the sour apple and ask directly, but fears he will *not* ask then, that he will leave without the money, go out broke and feeling lost and miserable. Bluett remembers how it was to be young. Not as much fun as generally believed and assumed and pretended. *Best years of your life, my butt,* Bluett thinks. *It's goddamned hard to be young.*

"If you need money, Tim—or anything at all, you only have to ask. If I can help you, I'll be glad to." Will you reach that far to me? But the boy is staring out the window, lips pursed.

Bluett swallows some beer, waits. "Been reading anything good lately?"

"Textbooks."

"Boy, you seem pretty down, Tim. You used to have so much fun with your buddies. I remember how happy you were when you got that apartment . . ."

"Yeah, and what if I lose it?"

"Lose it? Why should you lose it? Are you in danger of losing it?"

"It's not always so damn easy to come up with the rent, you know. It gets me down, I go around broke, everything I earn goes for rent and books and food, and I think to myself . . ." The boy looks down at the table but seems to be peering into an abyss. "I think to myself, what if I can't make the rent? What if I get kicked out? I'll be out on the street. I'll . . ."

"That won't happen. I won't let it. And if it happens, then you just come and live with me until we get you settled in somewhere else."

"You don't have enough room here, Dad."

"Are you kidding? I'd *make* room. You can't believe I would let you get kicked out into the street. You *can't* believe that, son."

Timothy's face is open and tender. "You would do that for me, Dad?"

"Are you *kidding*? There is no question, Tim. No question at all. Of course I would do it. With pleasure."

The boy's eyes are moist, and Bluett cannot believe that his own son would have the impression that he would not help him, would leave him on his own in such a situation.

"Thanks, Dad," he says, and his voice is thick. "Really. Thanks."

And Bluett feels a gratitude so deep he cannot see the bottom of it. Gratitude that these things managed to have been spoken. That he'd had the good fortune to get behind this demon and chase it off. "Listen, sonny, I came into some money," Bluett lies, taking out his wallet, removing three hundred-crown notes, and palming them to Tim. "Here, buddy, give yourself a night on the town. Have some fun. And listen, why don't you take a couple bottles of that beer in the refrigerator. And some of that ham and cheese there. Take whatever you like. And listen, why don't you come over one evening soon and we can rent a video? We can order in a pizza, make a night of it . . ."

*

70

The visit is soon concluded. They embrace at the door, and Bluett watches his son's shaven head disappear along the street in the darkening afternoon, cherishing the memory of the boy's voice when he thanked him, cherishing the thought that this one obstacle had been broken down. Maybe with just a little time they will get beyond this, wondering if they will ever be close again in anything like the way it was before. He knows other men with children older than his who assure him it changes for the better again later and he hopes for that, determined that it will be so. His own father died when he was eighteen, at a time when they were at least partly at odds, so no new level of being together had ever been achieved.

He still remembers the day Tim was born, all the hope and promise of the day. He and his wife were in bed, about to sleep, talking a bit, and Bluett told her some joke, got her laughing. It felt good so he told another, and her laughter turned to something else. The bed started vibrating with her body, and she said, "You better get me to the hospital right now."

Timothy was born two hours later, and the nurses rolled the bed out into the hall afterward so he and his wife could sit up together with the baby for a while. Little Tim there, with his light eyes open, seeing what?

Bluett went home alone and lay down to sleep but he couldn't. He couldn't stop thinking about something, about the baby's head. He thought it had looked kind of dented. He couldn't stop wondering if there was something wrong with it.

Next day he found the baby already in his wife's arms. She was nursing him. It took some moments before Bluett could raise his eyes to the boy's head, but when he did, there it was again. Dented. Why had no one mentioned it? The baby was deformed.

He took his wife's hand, and their eyes met, and Bluett smiled. "He's so cute," he said. "Cute head," he said, his pulse sounding in his ears.

"Yeah," she said, "they get squeezed out of shape from the birth. It takes a day or two before they're normal shape again."

Probably nothing in his life, before or since, had had such an impact of reprieve upon him as that moment. Perhaps it was what he hoped for now. A moment of explanation that would eliminate this partial, temporary estrangement, bring them together again as they had been all the years of Tim's childhood and early adolescence.

When he and his wife were separating, Bluett tried to explain it to the boy. Bluett and his wife by then could not speak to one another without bickering, and in the course of trying to explain how impossible the situation had become, he said to the boy, "It's this life, son. It's no life for me," by which he meant the life of bickering with a wife with whom he no longer shared any joy and who he could not make happy. But the phrase stuck out in his own mind, his own memory, as out of place, as ill-chosen. What might the boy have made of that phrase? He suspected the boy might have thought Bluett meant the life of the whole family, life with *him* and his sister. He tried to talk to him again about it, but the boy cut him off, would not allow him to explain anything more, and still, a year later, they had not come beyond that point.

He stands now at the window and watches the corner around which his son disappeared and looks back in one sweep over his life, and he knows that he cannot regret the things he has done, cannot regret his marriage, it had been necessary, it was his life, a big hunk of it, the main part, that which brought his children to life. How can you regret your life? He and his wife had made vows and broken them, but not without regret, and their love had soured, had worn away, but they had also grown together, and who was to question the fate that joined them, that produced two good kids looking for their own way in the world. Who could question or regret that? Chance turnings decide a fate you thought you had all of time to pick out for yourself. All of a sudden it's there and then it's gone, and what is left but sawdust shavings?

At the windowsill, he remembers Tim's voice—*Thanks, Dad. Really, thanks*—and wonders what kind of man he is, that his own son could think that he would let him get kicked out into the street.

7. The Crystal Ship

Alone again in the darkened apartment, he carries the empty glasses out to the kitchen and thinks about calling someone, but who can he talk to about what he feels now? He doesn't want to turn to Liselotte for reasons he does not comprehend. Maybe he doesn't want to show himself emotionally naked. His sister, perhaps, but he remembers Noreen saying to him last time they spoke, "This is going to cost you a fortune." He wanted to protest, but it was true, he couldn't afford it, his phone bill the previous month had been a killer. "I'll translate an extra page tomorrow," he had said.

"Do you have an infinite supply of pages to translate?"

He had laughed, but as he stands looking at the phone on its little table by the window he realizes that there is no one to call because the pain he feels just now is and must be something he is alone with, realizes it is something to embrace, one of the edges of loneliness, a truth.

We don't know, he thinks, *what knives we put in one another's hearts, mates, parents, children, lovers.* But he feels some edge to the thought that is of no use and with that realization feels it slipping from him. For many moments he stands there over the telephone table gazing out the window at the frozen dark blue lake. He knows that what he feels now is a gift of some sort, the edge of sadness, the sorrow at the core of loneliness, a place he will return to in the future to learn more from.

As the depth of the feeling levels up to the surface, and he finds himself away from it again, just standing blankly, the moment having reached the end of its circuit, the telephone rings.

It's Liselotte. "Hi?" she says in a tone of query. "Are you okay?"

The hair on his neck rises. "Why do you ask that?"

"I just got a feeling that you might not be . . . okay."

"What are you, psychic?"

"Was I right?"

"Listen, you doing anything? Why don't you come over for a nice post blue-hour highball?"

"We don't have to drink. I don't want to interrupt your day, but I have something for you."

He nurses a Stoli-rocks while he waits for her, then another, and halfway through the second he feels it doing its work in his brain, feels that crisp certainty of anticipated pleasure, feels that perhaps he loves her, cautions himself not to speak that word, realizes that if he were always drunk he would always love her for when he is drunk all that exists for him and all he exists for is the moment, the beat of blood in the wrist, the response of his body to hers.

He finishes the second Stoli surfing the TV, watches a bit of David Letterman, Jay Leno, Oprah Winfrey, Ricki Lake, Jerry Springer. Springer is in a serious moment at the end of his freak show: "Love is accepting," he says solemnly. "And you also have to accept the love that people offer. You have to drink their milkshakes." Bluett clicks off the remote.

On his way to the kitchen to freshen his Stoli, there is a knock at the door. He opens as he passes and kisses Liselotte's mouth, her brown eyes bright as amber lamps with surprise and pleasure. He caresses her round full breasts, murmurs, "I want to drink your milkshakes."

Instead of a drink she asks for juice, so he takes a club soda to slow his progress. He sits on the sofa beside her, stirred. He wants her, but she takes something from her bag and holds it out to him. A large white jagged crystal, the size of a coffee mug.

"This is for you," she says. "You don't have to believe me if you don't want, but *it* told me you were feeling sad. That's why I called and asked how you were."

He takes it in his hands, cooling his palms with it.

"Close your eyes," she says. "Feel its energy. Let it in."

Despite himself, he feels something coursing faintly into his hands, his arms, his veins. Then he thinks that what he feels is nothing more than his blood.

"I didn't realize you were into crystals," he says, feeling vaguely disappointed.

"Something happened to me when I was twelve . . ."

74

Bluett chuckles. "Something happened to everybody when they were twelve."

He sees annoyance flash in her eyes, but she governs it. "You don't have to believe me," she says, and he is sorry for his flippancy, tries to turn it to humor, warmth. He holds the crystal to his ear. "So this here rock told you I was sad, did it?"

"It has been scientifically proven that crystals have innate energy," she says. "Why do you think they used crystals in radios? They channel through you, and then you are like the radio receiver. You tune in to the energy, which enters your body and comes out your hands. Crystals have intelligence. They attract certain energies that can channel to the higher self according to the person's aura, and, for example, cure a disease or close the separation from the soul essence."

"The soul essence," he says.

"When I was twelve I made a decision that I was a have not," she says. "I did not realize, or I forgot, that I was connected to God, but I found the way back with crystals."

"With crystals." As he sits there listening to her amiable nonsense, he feels a mild gentle warmth running through his body, filling his heart, his brain, his eyes, and he watches her, smiling, and realizes that this is not about love, this is about friendship and pleasure and a certain healthy skepticism of human motives, including one's own.

Crystals indeed.

He stands to get a drink, but goes to the window instead, and just above the lake, in the black starry sky, he sees the Hale-Bopp.

"Look!"

He remembers reading about this in the papers, in *Newsweek*, that it had last been seen from earth 4,200 years ago and would not be seen again for about another 2,400 years. The reporter for some reason had referred to it as "a frozen dirt ball," and Lars at the Booktrader had said, "*He* sounds more like the frozen dirt ball there."

Liselotte stands beside him watching it through the window, and he realizes it could mean nothing or it could mean something; it might all mean something, everything, that crystal, our eyes, our lives, every moment we spend together, every word we speak, right up to the last breath we draw into our lungs and release. *Maybe*, he thinks, *there* is *something*. *'Cause without something, there's nothing.*

On Friday she is free from work; having caught up, he doubles his page quota the day before so they can spend a three-day weekend together.

Thursday, just as he's finishing his tenth page of the porcelain exhibition catalog, there is a knock on his door. Sam Finglas. Bluett invites him in, pours a cup of coffee. Bluett notes Sam is unshaven. The skin beneath his eyes is pouchy.

"Had another call from your ex, Sam?"

He shakes his head, distant, yet somehow Bluett feels he wants something. "You want to talk, Sam?"

Finglas looks at him, and his eyes send a message that reaches deep into Bluett's heart but that he cannot comprehend, a gaze that will imprint upon him.

"What can I do for you, Sam? You got money trouble? Trouble with the woman friend?"

Sam only stares, sighs. "I got to go, Blue." He puts out his hand, and they shake, formally, and Sam holds on to Bluett's hand for several moments, staring into his eyes as though from very far away.

A chill touches Bluett. "Sam, I'm here. Right across the hall. Just knock on the door. Any time."

He nods, looks at him a moment longer, raises his palm in parting and is gone.

Bluett sits at his desk with Sam's eyes still in his mind. That stare. Startled blue eyes peering deep, but for what? At what? Conveying what? As though he were saying, *Read my eyes.*

Tell me, Sam. I can't read your eyes.

Or as though he were trying to read something in mine.

He sighs, goes back to his tenth page, finishes it off, checks it, prints it out. He makes up the bill for the week's work and clips it to the translation, copies the job onto a disk, and packages it all into an envelope, which he weighs on the postal scale. He licks stamps and sticks them to the corner, three carmine images of the face of Margrethe, queen of the social-democratic Kingdom of Denmark.

Then he showers and shaves, pats himself down with the new after-shave Liselotte bought for him, trims the hair in his ears, his eyebrows, his mustache, dresses, and pulls on his coat to take a walk down to the mailbox.

In the hall, he pauses outside Sam's door, remembering that gaze. He knocks, knocks again.

Nothing.

The weekend with her lies before him like a little paradise, Thursday evening to Sunday night, an island of pleasure. They are to meet at the Café Europa on Amagertorv, and his step is light up to Frederiksborggade, past Israels Plads, where earthy women in tight slacks hawk vegetables and fruit, across Nørreport to Købmagergade.

The streets are full of end-of-the-day office people out to shop, meet for drinks, dinner, and it occurs to him he is beginning to feel a part of it all again, after how many weeks, months of estrangement?

Since the divorce. Something he does not want to think about. The connection to someone, the breaking of connection. He has had his life. He passes a bakery, window display of petits fours and *wienerbrød* (Viennese) Danishes, and remembers sitting drinking beer with Sam on a sunny autumn afternoon. The wasps had been at their beer and on the butter and the jelly in the *wienerbrød* on the next table, and Sam had said, "Those wasps are like us. Their work is done, their queen is dead, the hive is gone. They have nothin' to do now but take what pleasure they can get from the little time left before they freeze to death or get swatted out. They want sugar, and they're mean 'cause somehow they know they got nothin' to lose. No purpose. Nothin' to do but fly around and look for sweet stuff."

He has had his life. His kids are grown, and the connection to Jette was a dead end. How odd it seems to him, to have spent twenty years of his life, the central twenty years perhaps, on a dead end. The kids, of course. It was for the kids, and they had turned out well, even if Timothy had not forgiven him yet. Time. They need time. Yet time is a sea that stretches in more than one direction. Memories wash up sometimes, late at night, on a lonely afternoon, of hopeful times, the times after they managed their first adjustment together, when they were a team in the world, part of a net of family. Her family really. His so many years dispersed.

He remembers Jette once saying to him, "You're my best friend."

He cannot recall the context, only the statement, how it surprised him with delight and warmth, an unexpected revelation of tenderness through her normally guarded exterior. Other moments, too. Their month roaming the desert in a rented Ford; last fling before having children. Swimming at sunset in a motel pool in a little town in New Mexico. Both of them brown from the sun and trim and wanting nothing more than to be together, talk, share their thoughts, make love, make babies.

Those moments too few. The failure was there from the start, too, a breach inevitable, only a matter of the destruction of their marriage waiting for the right moment.

Oh, they're still friends, but only in extremely small doses; otherwise the emotional poison begins to leak out. There would be no growing old together, no death do us part, no better or worse left. In the end, there had been only worse and worse.

And that was your life, Bluett. You chose poorly. Or behaved poorly. Did not have the stuff it takes. You have your kids but they are cheated of a family base. They have you, they have Jette, what little remains of Jette's family, mostly people in their late seventies, early eighties. Whatever became of the old family stretch where there were aunts, uncles, cousins, siblings? What is there now? What chance left? Yet that had been precisely his problem—that there had been *too much* family, too many in-laws, no other life. *Remember that!*

Passing the post office, a bright-faced couple catch his eye, arms slung over each other's shoulder, strolling through the evening rush, and it occurs to him he could start over. He could pick a new partner. He could have a life. Pick more consciously this time. Commit himself. Be joined again, this time knowing something about the place.

He follows Købmagergade out to Amagertorv, the Café Europa there at one side of the three-cornered square, the parliament across the canal, and he thinks of Liselotte sitting there waiting for him, knowing somehow she has already arrived. He thinks of the pleasure they have shared these past weeks. He has told her clearly that he is not looking for love. He wants a friend. He wants to have fun. He wants to live free. She understood. She agreed, accepted. He tries to remember whether she told him what she wanted now with her life. She is twice divorced, two daughters in their mid-twenties, alone again for how long now?

Does he love her?

She believes in the intelligence of crystals.

And the two of them, years earlier, had blithely been unfaithful to their spouses. Together. Well, perhaps blithely was too harsh a word. It was not without regret. Not without joy either, for that matter, ecstasy even. No love at home.

He climbs the steps to the glass door, sees her lift her face from a table by the big plate window that looks across to the parliament, and he becomes aware suddenly of Denmark, this country, of Danes, people with a shared heritage of traditions, a thousand-year history, and him an expatriate from a country not two and a half centuries old, cut off here from his past, nose at the window of something he cannot have and does not want.

Well, what then? What are you then? You'll never be a Dane. And you're not American anymore.

He does not break stride crossing the floor to her as these thoughts wallop him like a sudden gust of wind, cut the breath from him.

She smiles, stretches across to kiss him as he sits, a proprietary gesture. He almost draws back, but brushes her lips (less says more) and draws away under the guise of settling in his chair, his thoughts moving too quickly to examine or even to hold for later examination, everything moving so quickly, time like water, a flow of drops, instants. His eyes focus on the glass of red wine on the table before her. "That," he says, "is exactly what I want," signals the waitress, glances back at Liselotte, his eyes deflecting from her neck, the sag beneath her eyes, to her pretty mouth, her breasts, her Wild Turkey–brown gleaming eyes.

She puts her hand on his. He squeezes, takes it away to go for his wallet as the waitress brings his wine, and he empties his glass in two swallows.

From the Europa, they stroll down Østergade to Hvids Vinstue, the oldest bar in Copenhagen. They sit in the evening crowd at rough wood tables in the basementlike interior. He switches to beer, big schooners of draft, and is easy with her closeness now. "Think of all the drinks that have been served here, all the people that have come here all these, what? two hundred fifty years this place has been here. More than that. Two hundred seventy."

She smiles, playing the game, imagining. He tries to picture the place, say, one hundred years back, jowly men with muttonchops, a beer for a copper, talking of what? A century, no, more than a tenth of the history of this country, his own ancestors just settling in New York from Waterford, just beginning to mingle in the melting pot.

"Where shall we eat?" she asks, her eyes reaching for his, her glance telling him he is far away and she is calling him back.

"Are you hungry?"

"I will be."

He looks at her face, and in his reverie of time remembers that she is a few years older than he. Four or five years. He looks at her neck, sees the years there, swallows more beer and glimpses her delicate hand on the table, so perfect, like her feet, painted nails that turn him on, twenty of them, color of peaches, like her lips, kiss the toes, lips, fingers, nape of the neck, not the throat, not beneath the eyes. Yes, kiss all of her.

Eat the peach.

He picks her hand up from the table, turns it over and places a kiss in her warm palm, puts his tongue there, sees her pale brown, Wild Turkey eyes gone tender, touches her nose, says, "I don't like that look in your eye."

"What look is that?"

"Like the look of, uh, love, or something sticky like that."

Now they flash, and he chuckles, "Better." And, "What should we play now?"

They eat on Grey Friars Square, at Peder Oxe, a prime cut served by the sweet blonde hands of a cute young waitress. Bluett looks meaningfully across the table at Liselotte. "Her?"

She smacks her palm at him.

"No?"

Falling into the game, she shakes her head. "Too young and innocent. I want someone more sophisticated."

They finish with cognac by the fireplace downstairs in the bar, and he considers telling her about his experiences with Benthe and the sister-in-law. Then thinks, *what's the point?*

They take the few steps up from the bar to the dark square. He stands there buttoning his coat, glances at the fountain in the center, the green copper pissoir off to one side, dungareed legs of a pisser visible beneath the bottom edge of the half wall, at the ancient chestnut tree, huge and sprawling with bare wooden winter arms, twig fingers pointing everywhere.

"You know this square is older than my country," he says, and he remembers then all the summer afternoons he had spent here with his wife when they were young, the first summer they knew one another. To blot out the thought, he reaches down to lift the hem of Liselotte's long wool coat, splays his palm over her bottom and squeezes. "May I be so forward?" he asks.

"Oh yes, you are wery velcome," she says in shaky English, and he gets under her skirt then, but she ducks aside. "If you start that we have to go home right away," she says, "you make me wet."

He kisses her, delighted, thinking, *Yes!*

They stroll across the square to Skindergade, and at just that moment, a taxi comes along with its green *fri* light lit. Bluett says, "Talk about your synchronicity," lifts a finger and it stops.

"Where are we going?" she asks.

"Let's go to Christiania. Have a joint. Hear some jazz."

"I don't do that," she says. "I don't do any joint."

"You can have red wine there. The JazzKlub is great."

The driver throws the meter, turns around and cuts across the edge of Kongens Nytorv, past the big front of the Hotel d'Angleterre, Magasin du Nord, the illuminated face of the Royal Theater. Bluett cranes out the side window as they pass the door of the Satin Club. "Look at that," he says. "Look, you ever see that?"

"What?"

It is already past. He shakes his head. "Nothing." They roll past the old Stock Exchange, the Mint, over Knippels Bridge through Christianshavn, the Inuit statues on the square, and up Prinsessesgade to the gate of Christiania.

They pay, get out of the cab, cross beneath the wooden arch on the other side of which it says YOU ARE NOW ENTERING THE EUROPEAN UNION, through an alleyway to come out on the muddy dirt streets of the Free State, mud and ruts frozen now in the winter dark. Liselotte clings to Bluett's arm.

"Scared?"

"Stay close," she says.

"It's like the Wild West or something. A third-world country. But it's safe."

At the corner, a man in paint-spattered clothes approaches them, his arms floating around him. "You with the group?"

She tugs Bluett's arm to keep moving, but he recognizes an accent. "Where you from?" he asks the man.

"Me?" Arms lifting and falling and floating in the air. "From heah. I'm the Ministuh a Tourism. You with the group?"

"You're from Brooklyn," says Bluett.

"You could heah that?"

"You bet I could. Went to school there. How'd you end up here?"

"This is the *only* place, man. I been heah since the start."

"I read in the papers you got the bikers out, got rid of the hard drugs. How'd you do that?"

The man's arms float down to his sides. "We got the hard drugs out, but I don't know about the bikers. Sometimes I think they're still heah. Decisions are made on higher levels than I evah see. I don't ask no questions. Long as no one's kickin' ass and no one's selling that nasty shit, it's okey-dokey with me. I tell you what," he says. "You come in heah and ask for crack or snow or horse, they take your money and strip you naked and throw you right the fuck out on the street. It's like hahd love, you know."

Liselotte pulls at Bluett's arm.

"So look, you with the group or what?"

"What group?" Bluett asks.

"The *tour* group."

"No, sorry, nice talking with you, Brooklyn. Catch you another time."

They continue down the frozen mud of the road.

"Let's go," she says. "I don't like it."

"No, really, it's safe, it's great." It looks like the third world. No hash stalls are open on Pusher Street this cold, dark night so Bluett leads them into the little square of market stands, old hippies selling chillums, roach clips, glassine envelopes of five joints for a hundred crowns.

He stops at one stall, chats with the vendor, a man his own age, maybe younger, with a Fu Manchu and burnsides.

"These joints any good?"

"Don't roll 'em myself, but they're from a prime supplier."

"You vouch for them?"

He raises his palms. Could mean anything. They stroll to the next stall. "These joints make me high?"

"Prime shit, man. Classic."

Bluett asks for five and pays his hundred crowns. They continue down Pusher Street, which usually has a gauntlet of hash stalls where they sell cigar-size joints and baggies by weight, satisfied customers sitting around garbage-can fires toking happily away. Too cold for that tonight.

"I don't know about those joints I bought," he says.

The JazzKlub is closed and shuttered. On the next street, they hear music, Crosby, Stills, and Nash's "Suite: Judy Blue Eyes" blaring through the speakers of Café Woodstock. The lights of the bar shine on the dark street. Liselotte holds back; he tugs her gently. "Come on, you'll love it."

Inside is loud and warm and crowded. People sit at tables of four or eight in a long row. The bar is deep with bodies. Bluett buys a bottle of red-label Christiania pilsner and a small bottle of red wine, and they find a place to stand near the toilets. There's a little shelf on the wall where they can set their glasses and their elbows.

At the table across from them an Inuit man sits sketching. He sketches a fighting cock, fills in the background, tears the sheet off his pad, begins to sketch a boat. His hand never stops moving. A young woman beside him takes the fighting cock sketch and goes to Bluett with it, asks in English, "You want to buy a genuine Inuit drawing?" Her face is thin and lined and a tooth is missing on the side of her mouth.

He shakes his head with a smile. She sneers, sits again; the man's hand is still moving, filling in the lines of the boat.

Bluett and Liselotte chink glasses. She lights a Prince, and he reaches into his pocket for the joints, comes out with a coaster on which is printed a number, a name. He peers at it through the smoky air, sees the name Birgitte, shoves it back in his pocket, goes into the other and locates the glassine envelope. The joints are fat, suspiciously so. He lights one, draws deep, holds it for a second before he coughs. "Out of practice," he says tightly, draws again, does better, holding it. He feels a mild buzz he thinks, drags again.

Jim Morrison is singing now. "The Crystal Ship." And Bluett listens to the eerie sound of Morrison's voice, the strange lyrics, wary of the combination of those lyrics and the smoke.

There is a little space on their shelf, and someone puts his beer on it, a short, lean man with a ponytail and beard, pale blue eyes, a gentle face. Straight out of the sixties, but he couldn't be more than maybe thirty-two. He's drinking snow beer, smiles at Bluett, who raises his bottle in salute. It's empty. Liselotte's glass is empty, too.

"Want another one of them?" he asks the hippie, pointing at his snow beer even though it is still full.

"Well, I wouldn't say no," he says in the vaguely cockney English some Danes pick up. "*Tak.*"

Bluett has a soft spot for Danish hippies. He buys the round. His joint has gone out so he lights it again, tokes, passes it to the hippie, who tastes it, smiles apologetically.

"No good?" asks Bluett.

"You high?"

Bluett thinks, takes stock. "I'm jammed but I don't know if I'm high. Probably just the juice."

The hippie takes out a little knife. "May I look at it inside?"

"Go ahead."

The man squeezes the cigarette out between his fingers, slits the paper. Bluett notices three fingers are gone from his left hand, from the knuckle. He parts the tobacco inside, says, "You got three seeds there, that's about it."

Bluett peers, sees three green seeds amid the ordinary red-brown cigarette tobacco. Finest Turkish and domestic blend.

"Burnt agin," he says and drinks some beer. He has snow beer now, too. Strong and bracing in his throat.

"What's your names?" the hippie asks.

"Marianne," Liselotte says, and Bluett laughs. "I'm Blue."

"Blue?" The hippie smiles, reflecting on the sound. "A good name. I'm Ib." Ib takes a bag from his pocket, removes a thick strip of hash. He lays the hash on a scrap of foil, begins to cut it up, telling about himself while he works. He is thirty-eight, married, has a son who's ten; but his wife has left him because she thinks he is a bad influence on the son. He has a pension he got from the gherkin factory in Holland where he lost his fingers. He laughs. "Someone got a freaky surprise in their jar of gherkins." He scrapes the hash into a chillum. "I love my boy," he says. "I don't bother no one. I got to see my boy. We have it good together." He lights the pipe, offers it. "Marianne?"

She shakes her head, but Bluett takes it, and one toke sends him through the ceiling.

Led Zeppelin is screaming now, about getting back to rock and roll, been a long time, long lonely lonely lonely lonely lonely time!

Bluett takes the pipe again, sees Liselotte's face, knows he must not accept the pipe next time. He's as high as he ever needs to be, up where nothing can touch him, not even a thought, not even a memory. He wants to try to explain to Liselotte that if she just takes a hit or two, they will have the best, *best* sex she has ever known in her whole life, her hole life, but his tongue is not inclined to formulate words just now. He lifts his snow beer to his mouth to wet it, and an eternity passes as the bottle clears the shelf, floats up toward his face. He smiles, all the time in the world between the simplest of gestures.

"So cool," he says to his friend, whose name he cannot recall just now. "So cool." The three-fingered man snuffles with laughter as the snow beer trickles into Bluett's dry mouth, waters his parched tongue, his throat. "Oh, yes. Good shit."

The music is excellent, too. "Let's dance," he says to Liselotte, but she shakes her head. He sees fright in her eyes. She keeps glancing to the bar. Bluett follows her gaze. Four younger men stand with their backs to the bar, facing across the room to where Bluett and Liselotte stand. Two

Danes and two dark foreigners, maybe second-generation immigrants—and it occurs to him that what is he but a *first*-generation immigrant? They look very young to Bluett, like kids, his own boy's age. He doesn't want to think about that. He doesn't want to think. He feels the nose of panic seeking its way up inside him, remembers how a wrong mood can topple you when you're high, forces it down. He looks at Liselotte again, and words find his mouth.

"Hey, you got to relax and let be, sweetheart."

Her eyes soften. "What did you call me?"

"Marianne." He leans to her ear and whispers, "Liselotte," and what he wants to do to her, and when he draws back her smile is easy again, warm. Her blue coat hangs open, and he puts his hand inside it.

"I go to see my boy tomorrow," the man whose name Bluett cannot remember says. *Ib!* "We have one whole day together."

Liselotte's smile is sad watching him. There is too much sadness here suddenly. Bluett thinks if he could just take one more hit of the peace pipe he would be ready to climb on her but the pipe seems far away and there is too much sadness in Ib's beard, in Liselotte's smile. He whispers in her ear, "You want to go?"

She nods, grateful, and they finish their drinks.

Ib says, "I go, too. I go to my boy tomorrow."

They walk together through the frozen mud toward the gate. Bluett is thinking about the guy who sold him the fake joints. Twenty crowns, three and a half bucks, for a goddamn cigarette!

"Gonna talk to that guy. Tell him something."

Liselotte squeezes his arm. "What if he is one of those, you know. Bikers?"

"He was no biker. He's an old hippie, ripped me off 'cause he figured he could."

"No one know for sure," Ib says.

Wondering what Ib means by that, Bluett's high begins to climb again. He sees his feet in the dark, spattered brown shoes, gliding across the frozen ruts. A dog trots past, a mongrel with some Labrador in her, and Bluett calls to her, but Liselotte tugs at his arm.

There are people walking behind them. Bluett glances back for the dog, sees the four young men from the bar, moving four abreast across the frozen road as they pass through the empty stalls of Pusher Street. One or two are open now. Beyond, in the little square where he bought his joints, he sees that the guy he bought from has closed shop, a hundred crowns of Bluett's money richer.

That's a quarter page of translation, he thinks. But I pay sales tax and income tax on it so it's really almost double. Abruptly he becomes obsessed by the money, but a sound distracts him.

He can hear the shoes of the four boys behind them cracking against the cold mud as they move closer. He peers around him for an escape route if necessary, but sees no possibilities. Abruptly he comes down. Should have stopped at one of those hash stalls. He remembers vaguely there is a restaurant, the Flea, not far ahead where they could phone a taxi, but the taxi couldn't come into Christiania anyway.

The boys are just behind him now. He glances at Ib, who moves close to the wall of a long dark building they are passing, and it occurs suddenly to Bluett that Ib is one of them. Maybe they saw his wallet, saw him duped by the bad joints, figure he's some rich fuck slumming. To them, maybe he is. A wallet full of hundred-crown notes, a fortune to them. He spies a pile of lumber scraps along the side of the road, his eye searching for a plank he can use as a weapon, but his will locks. What can he do against five of them? Stay calm, reason, keep Liselotte safe.

Liselotte grips his arm as the boys come up behind him. Bluett hesitates, braced. The boys continue past, through the passageway out to the street.

Bluett's knees are weak in the aftermath. He wants to comfort Liselotte with a hug, but is embarrassed about the trembling of his arms. He says to her, "There's usually a cab outside."

"You take a taxi?" Ib asks. "I ride with you a little? Just up to the bridge. I can pay ten crowns."

"Sure, don't worry."

Through the passage to the little square outside, and a single taxi idles there in the cold, a Mercedes, green *fri* lamp burning behind the windshield, and Bluett heads for it gratefully.

He hears shoes on gravel behind them. The four boys waiting against the wall. They are moving toward them now in a wedge, a blond hard-mouthed boy in the lead. Bluett is thinking how incongruous the blond hair, blond whiskers seem for a tough guy, as he moves for the cab, shoving Liselotte before him.

The blond boy lunges and his fist hooks with a sharp crack into Ib's face, spinning him face down with a groan onto the hood of the taxi.

Bluett calls out, "Hey!" He has the taxi door open and shoves Liselotte in. "Lock the other door," he mutters and stands there behind the open door, staring at the blond boy.

The driver says back over his shoulder to Bluett, "You coming or not? Get in or scrub off," but Bluett is staring into the blond kid's eyes, glances past his shoulder to Ib.

One of the others, a dark-haired foreign kid, has Ib's arm. Then he punches him low in the stomach so Ib grunts, doubling over, as the dark-haired boy's knee rises into his face with a thump.

"You take it calm," the blond boy says in Danish to Bluett. "You take it completely calm. You go home now. You don't know this business so fuck off. Am I understood?"

Ib's face and beard are smeared with blood, but his eyes are calm as he glances across at Bluett, at the door of the cab, a vehicle of escape he just missed. One of the dark boys punches him in the side, and he grimaces with pain, then his face is calm again.

"*Så er det nu bedstefar,*" the blond kid says. "That means now, grandpa." He shoves at the door so it smacks into Bluett's chest. "I don't say it again."

Bluett is transfixed by the calm sadness of Ib's face, his silence. He hears himself say, "Yeah, but . . ."

The driver breaks in, "Either get in or close the door," and puts the car in gear. Liselotte is pulling at his arm. "You got to come now, *now*," and Bluett slides into the car seat, into the dark warmth of the interior as the door smacks shut, and the blond kid gives him the finger and kicks the quarter panel of the rolling taxi.

Bluett watches for a moment through the side window, Ib on the ground and the four of them over him, their legs working. Liselotte sits very still, unspeaking.

"Hey, you got a radio," Bluett says to the driver. "Call the police. Quick."

"Call what?"

"The cops. Call the cops."

"Why? It's just a Christiania thing."

"They're *killing* that guy."

"Who? What guy? It's a Christiania thing. The police won't come at night. They throw rocks at them and they can't see who does it."

"Jesus Christ, stop this fucking cab up here, you son of a bitch!"

Liselotte whispers, "No, Blue, we must get away, what if they come back."

"Stop the cab!"

In a bar across from Asiatisk Plads, the foreign ministry, he dials 112 on a pay phone.

They ask his name and the number he's calling from and his social security number.

"My social security number! There's a guy getting beaten, killed . . ."

"Stay calm, please, sir, we need your name, social security number, and the number you are . . ."

"Outside Christiania four guys are kicking his head in."

"We need . . ."

He slams the phone down. Liselotte sits hugging herself at a table, a glass of red wine before her. Bluett orders a double vodka on the rocks.

The bartender says, "They won't go to Christiania at night. Some people there throw rocks at them. They can't see them at night, can't see where they're coming from. I wouldn't go in there either."

Bluett looks into the man's face, a reasonable, middle-aged Danish face, Nordic, broad-jowled from Christmas pork and Danish lunches, frank friendly eyes.

"They were kicking this guy. Four of them. Kicking him on the ground. In the face."

The bartender shakes his head. "That's what they do now. In my day, they used their fists. Now they kick. They kick in the head. In the face. They use knives. It's from America, comes from America. Anything happens in America we get it here a few years later."

"These were Danes kicking a Dane," Bluett says.

"They see it in all these American films. On the television. Life means nothing anymore."

*

Another taxi comes to collect them from Asiatisk Plads, carries them back across Knippels Bridge and through the city. He tries to put his arm around Liselotte, but she is huddled into herself, stiff, so he takes his arm away and watches the night streets roll past, thinking about Ib, the son he should have visited tomorrow, the calmness of his eyes, the blood clotting in his beard.

Bluett considers the fact that he watched as the man's head was kicked and did nothing, knows he *could* do nothing, feels tiny and fragile here in this taxi, something less than a man, some kind of rodent that can only hide, only run. Dimly, in his mind, he sees himself hurting back, sees himself with a bat, swinging at the hard-mouthed blond man, feels his eyes narrow, his mouth tighten in a cruel smile. *Could I? No. Could I do that? No*, he thinks and stares out at the dark streets reeling past, uncertain what is happening.

Back at his apartment, he tries to turn the mood. "What we need now," he says, "is a little bit of *natmad*. Night food. And *"Eine kleine Nachtmusik!"* He puts Mozart on the stereo and butters a platter of open sandwiches on rye bread halves—salami and chives, liver paste and salt beef and raw onion, strong cheese. The aroma of the cheese hits his nose and he begins to salivate. He takes down snaps glasses from a shelf and lifts the aquavit bottle out of the freezer.

He serves the food at his oak table, pours snaps, beer. He lights candles all around the room, switches off the overhead light as the violins leap through the changes Mozart progammed for them two hundred years earlier. He closes his eyes, his head moving like a conductor's with the spring of the music as he munches, swallows, lifts his snaps glass.

"*Skål, skat,*" he says. "Cheers, my treasure."

She lifts hers, nods. "*Skål.*" Her voice is toneless, eyes flat. She eats half a salami sandwich, finishes her snaps and curls up on the sofa with her back to the room.

Bluett sits there in the candlelight watching her back, wondering where she is, what she is thinking. He looks at the platter of sandwiches, the frosted green snaps bottle, the beer. He carries the platter out to the kitchen and scrapes it into the garbage, shoves the snaps back into the freezer. He looks out the kitchen window at the dark backs of the houses across the little yard, sees through one window a big gray sheep dog asleep in a pool of light from the yard lamp. Up above, the dented moon hangs in the navy sky over the peaked silhouetted rooftops.

Bluett sleeps on the opposite sofa. When he opens his eyes in the morning, he realizes he was woken by the kid upstairs running back and forth across the floor. *Bump bump bump bump bump.* Turn. *Bump bump bump bump bump.* Turn back. *Bump bump bump bump bump . . .*

Liselotte is no longer asleep on the sofa. Across the room she sits at the table, dressed, warming her hands around a mug of coffee, looking out the window.

He clears his throat raucously. "Morning."

"Morn."

He rises, hunched to conceal his hard-on as he slips into the bathroom, pees, brushes his teeth, rinses his tongue with strong blue mouthwash, looks at his face in the mirror over the sink, guesses the time at 8:50, but sees by the kitchen clock it is already ten; overcast. The clouds had fooled him, curtained the light. He makes himself a cup of Nescafé, stands staring into the refrigerator as he waits for the water to boil, staring at the bottle of Granini tomato juice. His favorite kind. Perfect for bloody Marys.

Why not? They have the whole long weekend still. It's only Friday morning. He pours the steaming water over the Nescafé grounds, stirs, carries it to the dining table and sits across from her.

"Want a bloody Mary?"

"Good God, no, I don't," she says without looking at him.

I see, he thinks. *Let's say the world stinks today and it is generally my fault.* But he says nothing. Let her stew. He begins to consider alternate plans. Send her home. Take in a flick. Jerk off. Take a long walk in the Deer Park. Check out the bucks in winter. Take the train up to Louisiana and see the Picasso exhibit. Have lunch there looking out over the sea. Open cheese sandwich with slices of green and red pepper and a draft sounds pretty good about now. Snaps, too. Who knows, maybe the woman of your dreams seated at the next table, just waiting for you.

He sips his coffee, glances at Liselotte. *Oh, are you still here?* he thinks, amusing himself.

"Aren't you overreacting a bit?" he says. "So we saw something ugly. What could we do? What can we do? That world is not *our* world, we have no control over it, we can't do a thing but stay clear of it."

She looks at him. "What are we doing?" she asks.

I don't have time to talk about this just now, he thinks. *Can't it wait until I'm dead.*

"We're drinking coffee," he says.

Clearly she is in no mood. "You know what I mean."

"Well, suppose you formulate your question a little more precisely, hm?" *I've been through a whole twenty-year marriage of this. I'm not about to start taking shit from you just because we fucked a few times. You want war, you got it, babe.*

"What is the point of us together? What is our goal?"

"Now, I'm glad you asked that," he says, "because it gives me yet another opportunity to try to make things perfectly clear. We are together to enjoy ourselves. I didn't think about us having any particular goal. Except maybe to have fun. To please one another. To be close friends, the best of friends. Isn't that okay?"

She looks older when she's testy, her mouth unattractive in petulance. "Just for fun, you mean. You see me just for fun. We are together just for fun. To amuse yourself."

"Isn't that why you see me?"

"I'm not a just for fun girl," she says. "I am not just for fun."

"I'm not certain what words you want to hear from me now."

"Do you have other girlfriends?"

"Maybe I do and maybe I don't."

"Because I am not interested in getting AIDS."

"Oh, for Christ's sake, you know that half the time I can't even get it up anyway."

"This is not a joking thing for me. I have to know if you are using me."

"I hate these questions. I hate this conversation. It reminds me of everything I hated about being married."

"Will you be honest with me?" she asks.

He sighs.

"I am second to none with a man I sleep with," she says. "Who is Birgitte Svane?"

He thinks for a moment, then: "So. Now you go through my pockets, do you? This is moving fast."

"Who is Birgitte Svane?"

"None of your business; that's who." He thinks. "She's a girl I met in a bar and had a couple of drinks with." He is disgusted with himself for telling her that much. Should he tell that he kissed her? *Bullshit!*

"Will you be honest with me?"

"In another minute I will, but you might not like it."

"I vant you to be honest and tell me what is our future together."

"As far as I can see right now, on the basis of this exchange, we have no future at all. If you really want to push it to this point. Look, it was a pretty depressing night the way it ended yesterday. Don't you think you're over-reacting? We've been having a great time together . . ."

"You and Birgitte have a great time, too, maybe?"

He sighs.

"Thank you for being honest," she says. "I appreciate that." She carries her cup out to the kitchen. He hears the water run. Then she is standing in the doorway in her boots and woolen coat and Wild Turkey eyes.

He says to her, "You know, you are dishonest in a way you don't seem to understand."

"I am not dishonest. I am not just for fun."

And you're second to none, I know, he doesn't say. *So take a fucking hike.*

The door clicks shut after her, and he slams the flat of his hand on the tabletop so his mug leaps off and spills across the beige carpet.

"*Shit!*"

From the kitchen he gets a cloth and sponges cold water on the coffee, soaks it up, rinses the rug and sponges more cold water on, rinses. Then he takes a clean rag and scrubs at the spot. The stain is lighter but still there.

"*Fuck!*"

He flings the wet rag into the sink, goes out to the front window. Halfway across the frozen lake, the back of her long woolen coat is moving away over the ice.

"Stupid," he mutters. "Pain in the ass. Fucking liar!"

His stomach growls and he thinks of the sandwiches he dumped into the garbage the previous night, and he sits there, heavy-headed, in the dark morning, wondering what just happened, wondering whether he wants to crawl back into his narrow bed.

PART II

RESOLUTION

One thought can produce millions of vibrations . . .

—John Coltrane

8. Groovin' High—Aura Yellow

Instead he puts on Bird's "Groovin' High" and drops to the carpet, does push-ups, sit-ups, crunches, listening to Yardbird's fast fingers and quick breath as the sweat collects on his back, his forehead. He keeps moving, twisting, lifting, forcing his will onto his body until the desire to sleep, to crawl away, is gone, and he feels only the pull of his muscles, the course of blood beneath his skin. He works out until it hurts to lift, does ten more reps, then drops back onto the carpet in a wakeful rest, staring at the white ceiling, at the spidery cracks in the center, while Parker's sax melds into "East of the Sun."

The strings cannot belie Parker's expertise, and Bluett likes the number, but he reaches for the remote, flips back to "Groovin' High," closes his eyes and remembers flying over the Throgs Neck Bridge in an old Chevy one summer midnight, coming from a girlfriend's apartment in the Bronx, the satisfaction all around him in the hot night, hearing this Bird tune on Symphony Sid on the car radio. The cut ends, fades to silence, and he puts on *Aura*.

Behind the red-black curtain of his eyelids he listens to the strange symphony, moving through color to the rumbling, dramatic tension of "Yellow," sees some beast slouching across the frozen lake through the icy gloom of morning. And he thinks that the life he's living is one that he has chosen with every move he made ever since he was a child, every choice, every road taken or not taken for whatever reason, for laziness, fear, whatever. This is his life now. He is responsible for it. And it is not really so bad. He has food and appetite. He has shelter from the cold. He has a Persian carpet to lie on and a CD player and good music to listen to. He has nothing to complain about. Everyone is lonely. *Learn to be alone because you will always be alone whether or not you are with someone. There is still the possibility of kindness. There is still a possibility of being satisfied, however fleetingly; learn from your young years when you drove across a bridge from a girlfriend's house and heard jazz on the radio in the hot summer night. You don't have to understand everything. You can't anyway.*

For a few more moments, he lies there in the silence at the end of the CD, still hearing Miles's trumpet in his brain, listening to his thoughts. Then he gets off the floor and goes to the kitchen. He eats breakfast. Cheese, bread, blueberries in a small cardboard basket, brews another cup of Nescafé, which he drinks at the sink by the kitchen window, looking across to the backs of the houses on the other side. The big gray sheep dog is in the yard below, pressed up against the door, waiting to be let in.

Bluett reaches across the sink and unlatches his window to let some air in, and the dog turns its head, looks up at him with black eyes through gray fur, black round nose where the fur parts, and that acknowledgement from the dog, the welcoming shiver of his black nose, the vision of it; the thought produces what seems a myriad of vibrations in Bluett's spirit, and the vibrations become Miles, become Bird, become Trane, and trill in his nerve endings and for a moment Bluett is approaching ecstasy. Maybe he's still high—or maybe not. Maybe he's high on music.

He smiles, thinks for a moment of getting a dog. The door opens, and the dog trots inside. He can see it behind the glass of the door lumbering up the stairs, and he understands that what he wanted was *that* dog, that moment of *that* dog, looking at him, nose atremble.

None of these back windows is covered. He sees a kitchen, a segment of a sitting room with colorful abstract paintings on the wall, the corner of a sofa, a hallway. On one window ledge stands a clay flowerpot with a single red tulip on a green stalk. *I don't want flowers here*, he thinks. *Flowers need attention.*

And he remembers for some reason a Danish woman he once knew, briefly, who sought him out with her eye at a cocktail party and, when he answered the call of her gaze and approached, said, "You are a sexy von." They had no business being together, but he went home with her, and afterward sat with his head in his hands on the edge of the bed. She sat beside him, the two of them naked, still warm, and kissed his ear.

"You don't like me?" she asked.

"I do. You're fabulous. I just don't know what we're doing. I don't want you to get hurt."

With a wide open mouth and sparkling eyes she laughed in his face. "This is how you hurt? Then hurt me again, you sexy von."

"You know I'm married."

She watched him for a moment. "You know vhat your veakness is? All this guilty-boy stuff. Which do you no good because it don't improve you, it only make you not to enjoy vhat you like to do. Vhat you vill always do anyway, sexy von." Then she got up and pulled on a robe, knotted the belt with a sharp tug. "Go home to your vife and enjoy your unhappiness with her."

He couldn't even remember her name, only her body, chubby and graceful, her bright eyes in a round smiling face, a woman he never got to know. His marriage was already finished then in all but name, and it seemed no matter where he turned he found regret. But she was wrong. Just as Benthe was wrong on the disappearing cliff when she unknowingly echoed that previous woman: *you are a sexy*. But what is the answer, then? To bind yourself. Be a slave. To some "not for fun" girl. *It seems I should already know the answers to all these questions at my age.*

Down in the concrete yard space, a sheaf of discarded doors is tilted up against the dilapidated fence, weather-rotted wood, rusted hinges.

His sink is in front of the window he looks out of, and sometimes he stands at this sink brushing his teeth while a woman brushes her teeth at the kitchen sink across the way, one floor below. Sometimes she wears only a bra or is bare-breasted and the vision of her vibrates in his spirit, beautiful as the dawn, those sweet miracles of her breasts. But now there is no one in any of the windows. He looks from the one to the other of them, half a dozen still-lifes on a brick wall, empty, motionless.

He rinses out his coffee cup, thinks of Liselotte. His anger is past, and he begins to examine what has happened. He should have known better. Of course, he did know better but allowed himself to believe that she was not looking for something he could not give her or would not give her, something he has lost perhaps, or used up. Maybe it was just the difference between men and women. Or was he, in fact, using her? For his pleasure? Without a worry how it might affect her?

Am I a bastard? he wonders, frightened by the possibility. *Or only enmeshed in my guilty-boy stuff?* And he remembers his son thinking his own father would leave him out on the street. *But Tim and I worked that out. I reassured him. It is possible to resolve problems.*

From next door he can hear the feet of waltzing children stepping around the floor of the Kingo Institute of Dance for Children and the occasional barked commands of Miss Kingo, the stringy old turkey of a woman he sees on the street from time to time waddling about on her pigeon toes.

He thinks of the sheep dog looking up at him, nose quivering in greeting, of the bare-breasted woman brushing her teeth, and the sense of vibration of those images sings in his nerves and echoes back.

Emotion takes his stomach, and he hurries to the phone and punches in her number. She answers on the third ring, voice flat.

"I just wanted to hear how you are."

"Not well," she says.

"Oh." He waits. She doesn't speak. "Well, I just wanted to see if you're okay, maybe you'd like to talk."

"I am not okay, but I do not wish to talk."

An impulse flares in him to argue, to point out that he stated his position from the start, that she agreed, that she forced this situation. He smothers it. "Well, I just wanted to say that if you want to talk, I'm here."

"I do not wish to talk," she says.

He stands over the phone, looking at the gray plastic handset in its gray plastic cradle, joined by a coil of glossy black wire. A bizarre object that people talk through, from anywhere in the world to anywhere in the world, just like that, punch eight or ten numbers and you got the voice of someone ten thousand miles away.

Alongside the phone is the crystal she gave him. Intelligence, indeed! He takes it in his palms, cool and smooth. He thinks of radio crystals, channels a message to her, half-expecting the phone to ring. Then he smirks, returns the thing to the window ledge, but on second thought he picks it up again and chucks it into his bottom dresser drawer. Then he thinks once more— it's nice to look at, to touch, in a cool, desolate sort of way—and returns it to the window ledge.

Perhaps he should use the situation to get ahead of himself, work. A few pages of translation. Money in the bank. Earn money instead of sulking. But he switches on the television set as he passes it, grabs the remote and surfs.

On Eurosport, an enormous man in red tights is inside the chassis of a hollowed-out wheelless red car, carrying it red-faced along a track to a background of cheers. On CNN, a woman in a pink jacket says, "Today in Bosnia . . ." On NBC, Jay Leno's broad-jawed grin is eating applause. On MTV, a young woman with choppy hair says, "In a little while we'll be seeing viewer home videos!" On RAI, a beautiful woman smiles, speaking Italian. On France 24, a woman's beautiful face above the words EVE JACK-SON, CULTURE, says, "This is my favorite author at the moment . . ." On Danmark 1, the Pink Panther tiptoes down a corridor. On Danmark 2, a lumpy man stands before a weather map. On Sweden 1, a woman in a purple blouse speaks quietly in Swedish. On Sweden 2, a man in a state trooper's hat says with a flat midwestern American accent, "I perceived that the suspected perpetrator had entered into a Grand Union Supermarket . . ."

On Eurosport, an enormous man in blue tights is inside the chassis of a hollowed-out blue car, carrying it on bulging wobbly legs along a track while a background voice speaks with hushed strain, "He looks wobbly, but he is moving at a fast pace . . ." On CNN, the woman in the pink jacket is saying, "is not all glum . . ." On NBC, Jay Leno sits at his desk across from a very tall black man. On MTV, a man with green hair and a silver ball on his tongue flails his body in a frightening shadowy room to electronic music. On RAI, a woman on a stage in a low-cut blouse says something in Italian and seems to be listening to what the audience will say to her.

Bluett watches her face, her wide, beautiful mouth, sparkling brown eyes, her graceful, slender, broad shoulders and the vee of her blouse that draws his eye into the place where her breasts are wedged together in a beautiful valley of flesh. He stares for a moment, listens to her voice, tries to hear words, wonders if it is different to be Italian, to talk to a woman in Italian, does not quite know what he means, pictures himself with this woman, what would he say, how would she respond. The camera pans back and she walks across the stage in a close-fitting minidress, her walk a subtle dance, and he remembers a green-eyed Italian girl named Janine— Janine Belviso, beautiful vision—who was his first . . .

He kills the picture, sits thinking of Liselotte not feeling good, not wanting to talk. He thinks of calling her again, pictures her once again telling him she was not okay but did not want to talk, pictures those words hurting him again, pictures her using those words to hurt him, using his concern by refusing to allow it to contact her, holding him on the leash of his caring.

Then he sees himself thinking these thoughts and wonders if he is becoming a strange, suspicious, bitter man, wonders if he is being unfair, small-minded, tells himself to see it from her point of view. She got caught in her emotion, maybe thought she *fell in love*, and she had to know whether his feelings were similar and when they showed themselves not to be, she had to get away before she made a fool of herself, felt like a fool, or did things that made her feel foolish.

"To fall in love." He thinks about that phrase. It seems to him to describe a false situation, a forced situation, a setup where instead of two people being friends, a circumstance is allowed to be flooded over by the biological chemicals of romance that seem to promise something but only lead to a reasonless situation of isolated expectation and mutual frustration.

Love is a chemical.

Perhaps it is possible for two people to formulate, to enunciate, their hopes, to live reasonably together. He doubts it. It all seems so hopeless, fruitless. He has had his kids, has done his biological thing, *has* his kids. That part of his life is over; the kids are still part of his life, but now he wants something more. What, he wonders, does he want now?

He thinks back on the things he and Liselotte did together, the games they played. He begins to feel foolish. He remembers how they lay in the dark and played with the sex toy they bought, a game of assuming and surrendering power, a game of penetration, how he held her wrists trapped in his left hand while he penetrated her with the toy in his right, watched her face and played to what the expression of her eyes and mouth told him, worked it, playing with the power she had surrendered to him, that she wished him to use on her.

Then he penetrated her both ways and put his fingers in her mouth, and she put her fingers in him, and their eyes were locked together. It was not *sex* exactly, it was a kind of pantomime they staged, locking together their bodies in a bizarre embrace that signified a web of emotion that both thrilled and soothed and terrified them.

Who then had the power? Who controlled the game? We both did, he thinks and wonders if he understands it, if he *can* understand it, some part of him wondering if he is taking revenge on women in this way, another part feeling this is a passion deep-rooted in the play between man and woman, another part telling him to flow mindlessly with it, surrender to it, abandon himself, yet at the same time glimpsing frightening shadows somewhere along that way, around a curve.

Thinking now about it, about the fantasies they played with, the word games, the way their gaze would lock as they spoke, to relish with their eyes the revelation of hidden dreams, how quickly they had come to that, and for what reason? What had it meant to him and what to her?

That revelation and observation, was that *love* to her? Beyond the caring, *was* it love? What was it to him? He cannot answer.

It was a game, he thinks, though he cannot be certain that he was not aware of her caught in the trap of what to her was love and to him was a mere game with no consequences for his heart. Yet what did that phrase mean? Consequences for the heart? Are we such flimsy creatures? Eternal mooning teenagers? Eternally trapped in the well of our hormones? Don't we have the power to take control of these things so that we do not over and over again back ourselves into an emotional corner where the passion and the friendship are slowly corroded and eroded and destroyed by demands for a false, forced loyalty that . . .

The thought peters out in a dead end and he comes up against the wall of his ignorance. *Is it simply that I do not love her?* he wonders. *I certainly like her. I am attracted to her, feel passion for her, but in truth I do not feel a need to be with her. What does that mean? Is that not acceptable? Is it not acceptable to feel content in oneself finally, to maintain enough distance to keep from drowning in another person? Have I been unfair, unkind to her? Used her?*

One thing, he thinks, what he experienced with Liselotte was a quantum of difference from what he experienced with Benthe and Dorte. With Liselotte he was fully engaged. With Benthe and Dorte, beautiful as Benthe was, it was—what? Mechanical? Planned?

Unengaging? Lacking in intimacy. Yes, it was lacking in intimacy. He thinks of what she proposed with the sauna, the group sex. Was he just afraid of it? Afraid of letting himself go? No, no, that was not intimacy, not intimate, he thinks. That was strangers groping at one another, using each other. *To be intimate*, he thinks, *is what?* The word suddenly seems foreign to him.

Intimate. He goes to the shelf where he keeps his dictionaries, pulls down the Webster's, fat red dilapidated book, remembers how whenever he asked his mother what a word meant she would take out the dictionary and look up the word and often as not it would lead to another word and what began with annoyance to him became a closeness between his mother and him, became . . . intimate.

He smiles as he finds the word, reads the definition: ". . . belonging to or characterizing one's deepest nature . . . marked by a warm friendship developed through long association . . ."

That is exactly the word, he thinks, and he feels triumph, feels as though he has resolved a problem. With Benthe and Dorte it was the opposite of intimacy: Even though they were naked, even though they were crossing the boundaries of liberty with one another's bodies, it was not intimate, it did not involve their deepest nature. Whereas with Liselotte they were venturing into the deepest nature of one another . . . *Is that love?* he wonders. The word seems to cheapen their experience together.

He wonders if he needs help. If he should think about seeing a therapist. But couldn't it all be resolved with kindness, with intimacy and kindness?

He rises, goes to the kitchen for a garbage bag, returns to the bedroom and opens the dresser, removes the clear plastic box from behind his socks and looks into it at the flesh-colored toy they used to penetrate one another. How odd it seems now. He feels embarrassed, wonders how many people play with such things.

Years ago, he remembers, when he was a teenager, a French-Canadian friend of his named Marcel had invited several boys home once when his parents were out and had taken them into the parents' bedroom to show his friends something in their bureau: a dildo, large and molded with all the veins and contours of an erect phallus. Marcel had taken it into the bathroom and, sniggering, had shown how he could put water in it and squeeze the scrotum so a stream of water squirted out the glans.

Bluett had laughed with the others, but he had always wondered what it was for, wondered if Marcel's father didn't have one of his own, if he had been wounded in the war or something and had to use this thing in place of a real one. And where did people buy such a thing in those days? The one he holds in his hands now in the clear plastic cube is much smaller and is not molded to resemble a penis but is smooth and slender. A *butt plug*. Comic name. Why is the butt comic? If you got shot or stabbed in the butt it would hurt like hell, but still people would snigger.

He remembers, after using it, asking Liselotte, "Was it okay?" and her smiling wickedly. "I was in heaven."

He wonders where she is now, where he is, and he stuffs the box into the garbage bag and ties it shut, throws it into the refuse pail in the cabinet beneath the kitchen sink.

In the living room, he sits and looks at the walls where the masks he has collected over the years hang. One brass-plated one from Central Africa with two horns rising from the forehead, the eyes a straight dark line across the bridge of the nose, the mouth a short line below, full brown wooden lips. One from Papua New Guinea, black wood with white seashell eyes, red tongue down to the chin. He has read that that tongue is the emblem of a destructive god, like the Indian mask of Kali on the other wall, bulging eyes and fanged chinless mouth with her long carved tongue extending downward to devour the world, lap it up. He wonders if that is related to appetite, hunger, an interpretation of these things as a source of evil or destruction. Maybe when we desire, we don this sort of mask and become destroyers, he thinks, consuming others to satisfy our need. He wonders how this relates to him, whether it is relevant to consider removing himself from desire, separating himself from the illusion of the material world. He supposes that world—pleasure, ambition, desire—is an illusion of sorts, but considers that that supposition itself might be an illusion whose source is the doomed desire for perfection.

And still there was his pursuit of intimacy with Liselotte, the exploration of their deepest nature. That could not be wrong. That could not be illusion, that quest. But he realizes now with a certainty what he had only vaguely grasped about what Benthe was after: that it was and is empty illusion.

Intensely he becomes aware of his solitude, of his brain turning these words and feelings over and over in his mind. *Is this what is happening to everyone in the world? Everyone sitting alone and thinking? Or are they trying to escape this kind of thought with any mindless activity—with TV sitcoms, with porn, with pretense—going about and pretending not to be alone, when in fact they are alone. Aren't they?*

On the narrow corner wall hangs a long, white mask with thick black eyes and dark triangles extending down the cheeks beneath each eye— which his daughter once suggested were tears. Facing out on the wall opposite where he sits are the two most beautiful and frightening, the one a demon mask from Mali, a red-eyed jackal face with carved ribbed horns atop the skull, and beside it a white face painted with red and blue concentric circles, big staring eyes within black sockets. The eyes themselves are a corkscrew of circles that seem to draw one in toward their tiny black vortex.

This mask was very expensive, and his wife was angry when he brought it home and she learned how much money he had paid for it, but it was something that, despite how it frightened him, he knew he had to own, had to be able to see. He could hypnotize himself watching it, could feel himself entering another world, drawn out of this place of everyday reality into a place of wandering, perhaps—of wandering and arrival, perhaps— someplace very far.

He wonders now why these objects so fascinate him. *Is it because I feel that all faces are masks concealing what truly lies behind them? Or because I feel that the mask face gives greater authority and power to the tiny human creature wearing it? Is it because when we assume an attitude, we take on the character suggested by a mask—ferocity, desire, destruction, clownish mirth— and become that? Or is it because these powerful visages in truth have nothing behind them, are mere shells, dazzling lids upon the emptiness they cover, the emptiness being our maskless selves which only become something by our choice of action, which is the same as the choice of a mask?*

Also hanging among the masks is a North African flute carved in the shape of a phallus. He bought this at the antique market in Brussels because when he picked it up, not yet noticing that it was a phallus, seeing only that it was a flute, he had felt the blood rush into his groin. Then he saw what it was and understood its function and its power, to inspire. This powerful musical penis gives power and music to one's own penis.

He had been surprised when he brought this home at his son's reaction to his wife's repulsion. "You're *not* hanging *that* on *my* living room wall," she had said, and their eleven-year-old Timothy had shrugged. "Mom, it's just a fertility symbol."

He can understand, though, now, why his wife would not want it on the wall of their family room. It looked like something you might use as a toy. He wonders now if the artist who made it—how many years ago, in what African land?—ever used it that way.

Standing in the corner between the masks is his didgeridoo, one and a half meters long, a eucalyptus branch naturally hollowed by termites, painted brown and black with bands of white dots at the top, bottom, and middle, a mouthpiece of beeswax. His wife had also disliked this. "It's so drab. Only you would buy something that looked like that."

And in what ways did I drive her to rage?

He takes it up and sits on the floor with it extended on the toe of his shoe, fills his lungs and presses air through the hollow of the wood. The sound is deep, gently rumbling as an *om* chant. It vibrates in his limbs, enters his blood, calming him, like the chanting voices on Coltrane's *A Love Supreme*, in the second movement, chanting *a love supreme* again and again, like a mantra, like a prayer to whatever power is greater than our own, greatest in the universe.

He tries once again for a while to get the knack of the circular breathing technique that will make it possible for him to play for ten or fifteen minutes without stopping, but he cannot succeed in squeezing the air out of his mouth while drawing more in through his nose. Each attempt throws off the quality of the tone he produces through the wood, so he contents himself merely with playing for as long as he can release air from his lungs, perhaps a minute at most.

Sitting there on the carpet, he fills his lungs again and again, letting the air through the gnarled pipe in a steady, modulated flow that fills his ears, his mind, as he stares up at the vortical eyes of the painted mask, drawing him in toward their tiny black centers to the place of wandering he both yearns for and dreads. *A love supreme a love supreme a love supreme a love supreme . . .*

When his lips begin to itch, he puts the instrument aside. He feels calmer now; things seem more clear. *You were just bullshitting yourself once again,* he thinks. *Enjoying what she gave you of her body and allowing yourself to believe it was for free. And the end result is she winds up sitting at home feeling lousy and used and foolish. You should have seen the signs. Now all the pleasure turns to irredeemable sadness, all the intimacy to fake closeness.*

She hates him now, so he feels even more alone, feels the denial of whatever it is he *is*, its validity rebuffed. *You are not good enough. You will not do. What you stand for is unacceptable. You are a man cut loose from the society of men. You are alone, away from your own country, devoid of ancestors, removed from your family, from the religion you grew up in, working in solitude.* He considers these facts, considers himself considering them, rises above the consideration to think, *You are not unhappy, not really. You have nothing to be unhappy about. What is connection, really, but another form of illusion? How can you connect but as an act of heart and will from somewhere beyond the place of illusion?* Benthe, for example, her desire leaving him basically unsatisfied despite her physical beauty; he did not want to pursue her—emptiness . . . But isn't true intimacy possible? A meeting of two people's deepest natures? For a moment he believes he has arrived at some point of understanding, but at once it turns opaque again and the understanding, if it ever was there in the first place, dissolves.

He stands at the window looking across in one direction at the slanted peace sculpture, the other way at the neon outline of the chicken and the eggs, which are not yet lit, are now mere faint glass outlines on a brick wall in the afternoon sun.

He misses his children, the way they were when they were little, the sense of family the four of them had together. For a while. The sense of family when *he* was a boy, frosted windows in a warm living room in winter, the balmy air through screen doors in summer, the smell of honeysuckle, of cooking—ham, bacon, potatoes—a mother and father who believed in you as you did in them, brothers and sisters who were on your side—even though that is long gone. He still misses it at times. He even misses his wife, partner of his life for twenty years even though so much of it was sham and pretense, secret bitterness, bickering behind a charade for the children's sake, for the sake of maintaining the illusion that there really was such a thing as family, the cornerstone of civilization. *Maybe there is, maybe there was, maybe you have just failed. Both families failed, the one you were born into and the one you created, too.*

But the children are not a failure, he reassures himself. *The children are new lives moving forward in time.* Only the children make sense to him.

Across the lake now the building tops are in silhouette like houses on a monopoly board against a pink blue sky. He is thinking about his own parents now, about how long it took for him, living across the ocean, to come to terms with what he really thought of them, and he wonders if he has in fact betrayed their memory. His mother was so good and sweet she bored him, and he could weep at that thought, he could tear out his hair that he would think such a thing about the woman who had meant him nothing but love and support. How he wishes now that she were still alive and he could invite her to lunch—she loved to eat in restaurants—and sit and allow her to enjoy for a couple of hours all the empty meaningless chitchat that made her feel alive and connected. How he wishes he could think of his father as standing up clear-eyed on two strong legs instead of staggering across the living room floor and falling on his butt and sitting there dazed and groggy-eyed.

How he wishes he could think of his three brothers as something other than what they had been, troublemakers who went out picking fights in bars. Larry waking up one morning with two teeth lodged in his knuckle that he had punched out of someone's mouth. Sean, who did nothing but try to amass money, putting every penny aside, literally; even when he had a good job and went to work in a suit and tie, he would not pass a trash can that had an empty bottle in it without fishing it out for the deposit, picked up used newspapers off subway seats to save a quarter. Or Billy, who became a teacher at the local Catholic school and hit the kids, bragged about it, used a stick that he called "Clarence," threatening the kids that they would "have a chat with Clarence" if they got out of line, bragging and laughing about it to his friends. His next to oldest sister, Mary Ellen, had ended in an institution, locked in an obsession that her body was shot through with disease, that disease lurked everywhere, on the surface of every object, mixed into her food, her water. Sometimes medicine could bring her out of it for a little while, and she would be the person he had known as a child, smiling and tender, quick to laugh; but it never lasted somehow. Sooner or later, her eyes would begin again to take on that edge of terror, and she would begin to open doors with her handkerchief, to hold the telephone away from her face, to pick through her food with a fork.

There is only Noreen left. The only one he can still communicate with. She the oldest, he the youngest of the siblings. They cling to one another, feel they are the only reasonable ones, merely humor the others, who each seem so locked into their foibles; but who is really to say who is normal, who is seeing clearly? Could he and Noreen not just as well be locked into a *folie à deux*? Who is to say for sure that the others were wrong?

Yet at home they loved so fiercely, all of them, were all so dedicated to the family, they would kill for you, their love at home so fierce and unquestioning for so many years, insofar as outside threats were concerned, but what went on within the house was something else again.

How long it took him to see that, how he had to get so far away, across the ocean, to see finally how blind and mad it all was, the whole thing, the way they professed to believe in God and Christ, went to confess their sins, take communion, attended Mass and still were locked into all their petty madness, locked into a closed little house where they believed only in the infallibility of each other, and then each of them going out to start their own families on the same premises, to rear their kids to do the same hopeless thing.

The worst of it for him was that they saw him, young Pat, as their own messiah. The genius savior bound for glory who would light the way for them all. There was no way out for him but to run, run from people who loved him blind in their own blindness and get away to where he could breathe and shake free of them and, once he was free, to ask himself *why*? Was he better off now? What had gone wrong there with his people? Why *couldn't* he save them from themselves? Or join them? Just *be* one of them? Be of the time and place and people that had produced him? Unquestioning.

9. The Damned Don't Cry

There are at least forty-seven books on his shelves that he has never read, that he paid good money for and placed on his bedside table, then put up on the shelf and never opened. Or opened it to read a page, a few pages, then for some reason stopped and put it on the shelf.

It is only Friday afternoon of a three-day weekend that should have been dedicated to pleasure, and he still has the coaster with the telephone number of Birgitte Svane in Albertslund, where he has vowed he will never go again. Perhaps she would come to the city to meet him.

He considers this, sees himself with her in a restaurant, reaching across the table to touch her hand, admire her eyes, her throat.

Asshole.

You could as well call Benthe and go through that series of movements toward emptiness.

He stands before his bookshelves, eyes roaming over the multicolored spines, picks out a black one, a white one, a green one, a blue and black one, a flowery one, another white one. All books he has been meaning to read. Could make a pot of Irish tea. Or sip wine, nibble bits of cheddar.

He sits on the sofa with the stack of books beside him, holds a thick volume in his hands: *Close Encounters of the Fourth Kind: Alien Abduction, UFOs and the Conference at M.I.T.* by C. D. B. Bryan. He reads the epilogue: "When you have eliminated the impossible, whatever remains, however improbable, must be the truth." From Sherlock Holmes, in Arthur Conan Doyle's *The Sign of Four*. He wonders that a supposedly scientific study should use a work of crime fiction for an epilogue, sits considering that, gazing at the white page, feeling the vellum between his fingers, finds himself closing the book, taking another.

Allan Bloom's *The Closing of the American Mind*. He feels his eyes closing as he reads the preface. *The Loneliness of the Dying* by Norbert

Elias is appealingly slender. He begins to read with gusto but by the end of the second page he feels a door opening in his mind behind which is lurking an intense anxiety he is not prepared to face at this moment. He slaps the book shut, takes Castaneda's *The Art of Dreaming*, reads the first sentence, begins to wonder if he is in a state to read at all.

There is something between his teeth. He gets up for a toothpick, stands digging with it, staring at the lake. The sun reflects in the windows of a building across the way and back onto the ice in a pattern of nine glowing oblongs, which makes him almost think of something but he cannot remember it. He returns to the sofa, looks at the next book in the pile, Paul Johnson's *Intellectuals*, wonders if he ever *truly* had meant to read any of these books, or just bought them to support an illusion of himself as a serious man, goes to the next one, *Poems on the Underground*, leafs through, reading lines at random:

> When in disgrace with fortune and men's eyes
> I all alone beweep my outcast state . . .

> O rose thou art sick . . .

> A thing of beauty is a joy for ever;
> Its loveliness increases . . .

> They hand in hand with wand'ring steps and slow,
> Through Eden took their solitary way . . .

> Among them He a spirit of frenzy sent
> That hurt their minds and sent them with a mad passion
> To hasten their destroyer . . .

> Since there's no help, come let us kiss and part.

The last book in the pile he has selected is a translation of Dan Turèll's poetry. He leafs through it, stops at "I Should Have Been a Taxi Driver."

That's what I should have been!
I would have been a great taxi driver!
The cab driver to end all cab drivers . . .

He considers that, ponders whether, if he had chosen a simpler life, another life, his life would have been better. Still trapped inside the same confused mind, though.

Spinning through pages, he stops at random, finds one of his favorite poems, "Last Walk through the City." About a man taking his final walk through Copenhagen before he dies. Turèll wrote that in his thirties, imagining his death, but never imagining that he would be dead a dozen years later of a sudden cancer, not much older than Bluett is now. He thinks of Turèll, of Copenhagen, thinks of stopping in the Café Golden Rain for one last shot of bitter snaps as Turèll imagines himself doing in that poem.

The thought of drink has found his heart and he sits considering various bars, places where he might meet some drinking companions, remembers his encounter in the Bo-Bi Bar, remembers Milt Sever recalling Andreas Fritzsen writing things he did not wish to know about child pornography. He thinks of his American criminologist friend here in Copenhagen—Dave. Bluett phones him. No answer. His Danish-Czech friend, Per, a novelist. Tries him. No answer. Thinks of Sam across the hall, but no doubt Sam is with his Russian mistress.

Then he remembers that strange look in Sam's eyes last time.

I should have been a taxi driver, he thinks, carrying the books back, placing them one by one in their empty slots on the shelves.

In the kitchen, he takes tomato juice, Tabasco, salt, pepper, Worcestershire sauce, Stolichnaya, and concocts a pitcher of bloody Marys, which he carries on a tray with bowls of nuts and chips across the hall. He balances the tray on his hip and hammers on the door. "Open up, Finglas!"

He waits, hammers again. "Sam!" Hears nothing, no stirring. Silence.

Trying not to think of Sam with his beautiful Russian girlfriend, he returns, puts on Coltrane's *Complete Africa/Brass Sessions*. "The Damned Don't Cry." And his heart lifts that it is the perfect music to sit at his oak table with, sipping bloody Marys, nibbling nuts, watching the frozen lake get soupy in the gleaming sunlight.

What is light? he thinks, abandoning himself to the pitcher, the spice and 80-proof numbing of his lips and teeth. He nods to the great sax, smiling as the inevitable Coltrane disintegrations draw him down to where you see beneath the music, the machine room of sound, scary as hell but powerful as god and then the horn comes back to show you from the outside again, smooth hot beauty, bringing the two closer together, a marriage of heaven and hell.

Trane leaves off and Reggie Workman takes it on the bass alone before Booker Little's trumpet and Coltrane joins him on soprano, on oboe, tuba, and the rhythms swing out of this forty-year-old sadness cut into wax.

Bluett drinks his bloody, refills the glass and stares at Coltrane's face on the CD jacket, grateful to that dignified face for these sounds. He leans back, tongue numb now, stands and does a little dance, slaps his thighs, turns to the bookshelves, grabs Kierkegaard's *Fear and Trembling* and slams it back, his hand charged with the touch of it as Coltrane's soprano blows "Africa," lifting upward like a bird cry of thought. Bluett closes his eyes and smiles, leaning on the chairback, nodding to the rhythms.

He steps to the window, opens it to breathe in the icy air, gazes down one story to the bright, cold street. That gray-eyed foreign guy again on the corner. The unknown neighbor, standing aside in the freezing afternoon to let a young couple pass—a tall young man in a leather jacket with a woman, slightly older, who turns to smile at the foreigner, her blue eyes so light he can see their glow from here. "*Mange tak,*" she says with warmth, "Many thanks," and they walk on away from the man, who stands in a strangely twisted posture, as though he has back pain, and watches the couple for a moment as they disappear up the street, and Bluett experiences a spooky moment of recognition, of a constellation of four lives, trajectories crossing at this moment of Coltrane's soprano, continuing away.

Then a banging reaches up through the music into his consciousness. He moves to the stereo, lowers the volume.

Someone is in the hall. He shuts off the sound and looks out. A young man stands at Sam's apartment doorway knocking, hammering at the door. The young man glances back at Bluett.

"Have you seen my father?"

"You must be Anders," Bluett says. "Sam always talks about you. He's proud as hell of you." Bluett can understand Sam's pride. The boy is good-looking, well-dressed, an intelligent face. Bluett introduces himself.

"My father is supposed to meet me today. I was supposed to meet him here twenty minutes ago." The boy's English is accented, sibilant *esses*.

"Tried him before myself," Bluett says, "but no luck. If he was supposed to meet you, he'll be home for sure any minute. You want to come in and wait here?"

The boy looks skeptical.

"Don't you have a key?" Bluett asks.

"Uh, I forgot it."

"Well, listen, I can let you in. We hold keys for each other. Wait a sec . . ." He goes in and finds the key, which he has hung on a red cord beside the refrigerator, opens the door for the boy. "Give Sam my regards when he comes."

He returns to his apartment, his table, stares at the CD player, the red half-empty pitcher, wonders if he can revive the mood, if he even wants to. Then there's a knock on his own door this time. Sam's son again, but Bluett can see at once something has happened.

The boy's face is drained, frightened, the same startled blue eyes as Sam's. His voice is very slight.

"Someone has . . . killed him. My father."

10. Blood Count

The events of the day bring him down from his vodka cloud, but the chronology is jerky. Now he sits alone again at the end of a weekend, and it occurs to him that this is a continuous situation, fleeting days vanishing in a blur.

There was the boy Anders's stricken face. What had at first seemed murder later was seen as suicide. In the boy's hand was the note that Sam had addressed to him, telling about cancer, that he could not face a drawn-out eating away of himself, months of pain and dying and dependence, that it was better like this, that he hoped it wasn't unfair but that he wanted his son to be the one to find him, to find this note so that he could read it for himself, so he could say once more how much he loved the boy, how proud he was of him and of his sisters Annette and Mie, that they should not think harshly of him if they could avoid it, this way they were spared something much worse, that they should take care of one another and know always how much their father treasured them.

Bluett did not want to see Sam's body but wound up in the man's bedroom nonetheless, and his immediate sense was that something was more than wrong. The room, the apartment was tidy and clean, and there was a plastic bag over Sam's head. His hands lay on his breast with a necktie wound around his wrists. Bluett backed out as quickly as he could without startling Anders, who stood in the little hallway behind him.

Then the police were there, and Bluett waited for a moment alone with the dark-haired older policeman to ask about the bag and necktie around his wrists.

"It looks like he was killed. How could he have tied his own hands?"

The policeman's blue eyes glanced at Bluett and turned away. "There was no knot. It was just wound around his wrists. They do that sometimes to make sure that if they wake up, their hands aren't free to phone for help. When you're drugged, even just having something wound around your wrists might be enough to stop you, apparently. Just wanted to be sure nothing got in the way, not even himself."

Anders's younger sister, Annette, was at the door, a strikingly beautiful girl, movie-star beautiful, and it occurred to Bluett that Sam's ex-wife must be a real beauty as well. He had never met her and wondered if she would show up before the body was removed, but then another man was there, a doctor, and two Falck ambulance men with a stretcher and a body bag.

The younger policeman, with a scarred jaw, asked Bluett a few questions: Had Sam ever mentioned the cancer to him, did he seem unhappy, did Bluett know of other problems he might have been experiencing?

And Bluett found himself telling the policeman that Sam had told him about a woman he was involved with, a very beautiful Russian woman he was apparently in love with. They stood in the hall as they talked, and Anders, near the door of Sam's apartment, looked up sharply at those words, and Bluett hated himself for not being more tactful.

He glanced at the boy, tried to express his grief in a look, but Anders turned away. The policeman asked if he knew the woman, knew where she could be contacted.

"I never actually met her," Bluett said.

He did not mention that he had seen her once or that she and Sam had disappeared behind the door of the Satin Club. He did not know why he hadn't mentioned it. Instinct. A feeling that if he told, the information could not be taken back. But why should he want to take the information back?

Next day, Saturday, he hears more activity in the apartment, people talking in the hall, descending the stairs. He goes to the window and looks down to the street. A car is parked there and stenciled on the side is the name of the realty firm from which Bluett had bought his apartment. A moment later, two people appear through the gate and stand by the car. The realtor and Sam's Russian girlfriend. She wears a black raincoat and sunglasses, but there is no mistaking the beauty of her face. The realtor unlocks the door of his car and opens it for her, happens to glance up and sees Bluett there, throws a subdued wave. The woman glances up, lowering her sunglasses onto her sharp cheekbones, and for some reason Bluett does not understand he ducks back from the window, but not before their eyes meet.

In a box of papers at the top of his closet, Bluett finds the card the realtor gave him when he bought his own apartment here. It is eleven in the morning. He waits half an hour and makes the call, identifies himself, mentions he was Sam's close friend, asks if the family has put the apartment on the market.

"His fiancée did," the realtor says. "The apartment is in her name."

"*What?* What about the kids?"

"They were not especially glad about it. She was in here already yesterday afternoon, and the papers were in order. He sold it to her. For a song. I met the son once, Anders, and felt like I ought to give him a call. Didn't like to bother him with all that happened, but . . . Apparently Sam's bank book was empty, too. Even of the song he sold the apartment to her for. Nothing left but a small annuity the kids will share. Maybe forty thousand crowns apiece. They were not glad. But all the paperwork was in order. There was nothing to do about it."

"What's the apartment worth?"

"She wants a quick sale. She's asking one point eight. But she'll go as low as a million and a half crowns."

"Are you going to handle it for her?"

"I'm a businessman. That's what I do."

There is not much more of the weekend. A long, slow walk around the lake to watch the skaters on Sunday, a cappuccino at the Front Page and a stroll across Peace Bridge, where he buys *Politiken*, with which he spends the remainder of his afternoon, leafing slowly through the newspaper, a pot of Bewley's afternoon tea at his side.

He reads the news and the sports and the weather. He glances through the TV listings, reads the Nicoline Werdeline comic strip about a woman who is unfaithful to her husband, the one by Strid. Strid usually makes him smile. This time he is interviewing a penguin in the zoological gardens. The penguin has been sponsored by the Danish National People's Party and is irate. "They're racists!" he says to Strid, who shushes the bird. "You're not allowed to say that, it's against the law, you could get a fine for defamation of character," and the bird squawks, "I'm an animal, I don't have to obey that law. They're racists! Racists! Racists!"

Bluett chuckles, studies the drawing of the bird, begins to laugh, and the laughter takes hold of him so he cannot stop. Then he is trembling, staring with terror out at the frozen lake, fearing the emotion that wants to grip him. He breathes slowly, deeply.

It passes.

He turns back to the newspaper, reads the classifieds, ads for alcohol clinics, psychotherapy, clairvoyance, organic psychotherapy, spiritual advice, friendship, lovers, exhibitionist clubs, homophile/lesbian clubs, advice for men, the association of single fathers, astrological advice, self-help groups, S and M clubs, a support center against incest, an AIDS support group, a shelter for battered wives, an offer for cheap dental work in Sweden, for the association of transvestites . . .

Family paper. A Danish family paper.

On the last page is an ad for women's underwear, a black-and-white picture of a very ordinary looking woman in very ordinary looking white panties and bra, her body sitting on a blank background, her ordinary face lit with an ordinary smile, and he sits staring with longing at the picture for many moments.

Then the last edge of sunlight is withering down behind the unlit neon chicken and the tilted monolith, and behind the tall state hospital, and he refolds the paper and carries the cold pot of tea out into the kitchen and sees the gray sheepdog standing at the door across the way, waiting to be let in again.

This time the dog does not look up at him.

He takes a drink after all, Stoli on the rocks, hesitates for a moment, with the neck of the bottle over the rim of the glass, thinking of his father, but feels content his own intake is nothing compared to what his poor dad's was. Which makes him think of a joke he heard recently, from Sam, in fact: What's the definition of an alcoholic? Someone who drinks more than his doctor. He pours five fingers for himself, and puts on one of his favorite cuts of his favorite CD: Stan Getz doing Billy Strayhorn's "Blood Count," recorded live in Club Montmartre, here in Copenhagen, not long before the C took Getz. Bluett holds vodka on his tongue, smooth Stoli, and listens to Getz's tenor run the range of sorrow, of sorrow that is inevitable, unbreachable, thinks about the fact that Getz blew those notes in this city ten years earlier, four years before he died, wishes he had been in the club that night to hear it, wishes more, wishes to Christ Sam could be here with him right now, just for the four minutes and two seconds it takes for the melody to run through its last chord, Getz's voice saying, "Thank you." Then silence. End of the CD. Last number.

There are several things he regrets. That he did not get a telephone number for Anders and Annette and the other sister, that he did not invite them out to talk a little; even if they declined, he could have just asked them. He wonders whether Sam had many other friends, close friends. They both know a few drinking companions here and there around town. The two of them joined Dave and Per and Frej for pivos every other month at Fru Snorks alongside Enghave Plads. But who was there to give the kids a kind word now? His own situation is similar to Sam's. All these years living in another country, your own people gone, no more friends left from the home country, not even any colleagues; both he and Sam worked independently as translators. Just half a handful of occasional friends. The kids are cheated of half a family.

He realizes in a large sense it is his own situation he grieves over, but he grieves over Sam's as well, over Sam's fine-looking kids and the sadness they must face alone now, over the sadness of life in general, the sadness at the heart of things. Keep it comic; don't feel, *think*. Fall on your butt and laugh at yourself. Tell a tale about your sad times and laugh twice: Har. Hee.

He finds himself thinking about Sam's suicide then, about the taboo against it, how formerly Christians were refused burial in hallowed ground, how in medieval times they were buried outside town at a cross-roads, how even Buddhists judged that it invoked untoward cosmic consequences: Kill yourself and you come back instantly as a dung beetle.

He wonders.

What cosmic balance could the snuffing of a single flame disturb? Surely Sam had his reasons. Cancer. It is just difficult for Bluett to accept. Sam had said not one word about it, had been full of the light of infatuation for this woman—Svetlana Krylova, the realtor said her name was.

Fiancée? Sam had said he didn't want to marry. When could he have found out he had cancer—the day he had that look in his eyes?—and how could he have known or decided so quickly that it was hopeless and incurable? Some cancers are like that, though, Bluett knows. Dan Turèll found out about his throat cancer and died within months. In great pain.

But there is another question that won't leave him alone. When exactly did Sam sell her the apartment? He'd never mentioned a word about that, either. When did it happen? And how could she already be in the process of selling it? And given that Sam loved his kids so much, how could he not have left at least a share of the apartment to them? It was a roomy apartment, well located, with at least a partial view of the lakes, and a moody view out the back, and Bluett knew for a fact that it was paid off— worth a good two million crowns on the current inflated market, $350,000. Even a fifth of that to each of the kids would have given them some kind of start in their young lives. How could Sam have neglected that? And the "fiancée" was letting it go for a million and a half. Fast sale.

PART III

PURSUANCE

Charlie Parker leaning up against the paint shop's stone stoop
Charlie Parker behind the bar
Charlie there throwing a coin in the juke
look now Charlie's dancing to "The Great Pretender"
twenty years after his American death—

—Dan Turèll, "Charlie Parker on Isted Street"

11. Bad Religion

Into the dark comes the sound that drags him out. He reaches for the little clock to silence it, dozes, holding it in his hand, thinking, What day is it? Monday? Tuesday. *It is not good to let yourself sleep now*, even as he slides down into the cozy dark again.

There had been a time some years earlier, just after he finished high school, a period of two or three years when he was on his own, slowly realizing that now he was responsible for his life. He could do what he wanted. No hindrances. No help, either. His father was dead. He went to college at night and had a crummy job in a management trainee program at the Bank of New York at 169 Maiden Lane, near Wall Street. His friends had squeezed many a cheap laugh out of that address: 169 Maiden Lane. He was to start by spending three months in a series of departments, learning the details of the bank's daily operation.

At the time he is thinking of, he was in the Stock Transfer Department, he was eighteen, and his job each day was to put small white pieces of paper, stock coupons, in number order. This was long before the microchip. The numbers were red, printed in the upper right-hand corner, six digits. The lesson he was to learn was the extreme importance of this small, seemingly insignificant task being performed accurately every single day. There were thousands of stock coupons, each indicating a stock transaction, and if they were not organized so as to be immediately traceable, the entire stock transfer system could break down. This could happen very quickly, and even a one-day breakdown could cost the bank large sums of money.

Bluett's training director wanted Bluett to understand the experience of this task by *living* it for a time, morning to evening, day after day.

Bluett often overslept and arrived late for work, and his training director had a way of looking at him when he punched in past nine, a way of very slowly turning his face to gaze at Bluett while raising his wrist to his eyes to show that he was looking at his watch. He said nothing, but the message was clear, and Bluett, when he woke late in the morning, would be gripped by terror and loathing at the thought that he would have to be subjected to this performance once again.

His training director's name was Hagin—Mr. Hagin, he was supposed to call him. Mr. Hagin had large brown eyes, and his nose ran apparently without his being aware of it, so that there was usually a line of transparent mucus between one or both nostrils and his upper lip. Bluett dreaded having to look at him, dreaded his days, dreaded getting in late.

One morning when he woke late, the dread of being looked at by Mr. Hagin was so great that he decided he would play sick, stay home all day. He lay in bed waiting in agony for nine A.M. so he could phone in and get it over with, but once he had called and told his director's secretary that he had a terrible toothache and had to go to the dentist, he felt suddenly liberated. The whole day lay before him, free, a bonus, a paid sick day. He wouldn't even lose money for not being there. He went back to bed and read the newspaper, dozed, masturbated. He ate lunch in bed watching some old film on TV and dozed some more.

Finally, around four in the afternoon, he got out of bed, showered and dressed, went out for a walk, met some friends for a beer. When he went to bed that night he was not tired so he read for a while, but he still could not sleep. An hour passed, two hours, three. At 3:45 A.M. he was still awake, and he knew he would never wake on time in the morning, so he set the clock for nine to wake him just in time to call in sick again. He told Hagin's secretary that he had had a painful extraction of an impacted wisdom tooth (something one of his brothers had experienced once), and the pain had kept him awake all night, and now he had to go back to the dentist to have the operation completed.

Afterward he sat in his underwear on his threadbare secondhand sofa in his seedy little East Fourth Street apartment and saw doom smudged all over the grimy pane of his one window. What would become of him? What could he do?

Perhaps because the questions were so intensely felt in his heart, answers were produced from somewhere inside him. It was as though a door had flown open in his mind to reveal a slate on which were printed the words: IF YOU DO NOT GET UP EARLY AND WORK HARD, OTHERS

WILL LOOK UPON YOU AND SAY HE DOES NOT GET UP EARLY AND WORK HARD.

And then, the primary truth: YOU HAVE TO GET UP WHEN THE ALARM CLOCK RINGS.

From that day on, he had no trouble in his working life. The knowledge that he had no real choice but to rise when the clock beckoned him saved him from the chaos into which he had slowly been slipping simply because he had no argument against it, simply because the yearning for ease, for the cocoon and womb of sleep, had no counterweight to pull him free. Now he knew what the sound of the clock meant, why it is called an *alarm* clock: Sound the alarm! Danger! You are sunk over your eyeballs! Rise!

And now all these years later, for perhaps the first time in two decades, he wakes with a start, the alarm clock in his hand. He has gone back to sleep instead of rising. In panic, he checks the time: Only twenty minutes have passed. He is his own boss now, but then it is even more important that he have control over himself. Five pages a day minimum. To pay his bills, remain solvent, he must do five pages a day minimum on average per week.

Yet still he does not rise. He reaches the clock back to the bedside table and stretches, his eyes drooping, picking through the fog of his brain for something that seems to want his attention there. He is thinking about God, about what he ever meant by the word God, but he does feel that he has seen God—even if God or god is utterly beyond his ken—and he feels that he has seen the ungodly, and tries to sort through these thoughts, which are confusing him.

The word *God*, then, transforms in his mind into *the box*. Sam said something about putting a box in his storage room. Had he actually done so? Bluett has no idea. He can scarcely remember anything about it. What had Sam said? He had a box of things he wouldn't want anyone to see if anything happened to him. Had he already known something then? And what did he mean? Did he mean for Bluett to destroy the box if anything happened to him? Did he actually say that? And if he did, what would Bluett do? Should he just destroy it? Could he? Was it legal? Should he try to contact Sam's kids, his ex-wife, give the box to them? But that must be precisely what Sam was trying to avoid if he put it in Bluett's basement room.

He throws off the covers and sits on the edge of the bed, thinking about the storage room, but he rises and crosses to the bathroom, past his little work room, and glimpses the neat stacks of paper on his desk, awaiting him. He is already half an hour late. He thinks of how Hagin would have looked at him for coming even ten minutes late. Half an hour!

Thinking about Hagin, Bluett realizes that was almost twenty-five years earlier. Hagin would be . . . how old? Must've been at least forty then. So he would be sixty-five now. Retired. An old dude. Probably with a good retirement plan, too. Which Bluett could not say for himself.

Standing there on the living room carpet, he stares blankly at the masks on the wall, the didgeridoo, thinking about the basement, the storage room.

No.

Five pages.

He shaves, brushes his teeth, dresses, carries a glass of juice to his desk, and looks at the new projects that arrived in Saturday's post: a series of articles for the personnel newsletter of a Danish drug firm that has gone international. The first article, nearly done, seven pages long, is titled, "The Joys of International Exchange." Clearly the aim is to loosen people up to the idea that they may be called upon to move to one of the company's other departments in England, Thailand, or the Philippines.

Bluett reaches for the red Gyldendal Danish-English dictionary on the wall shelf above his desk and gets to work.

He translates in pen on a yellow pad first, doing a literal translation, which he then keys in on his laptop, turning the sentences away from the Danish idioms into purer English equivalents, studying each phrase carefully to be certain he has not semiconsciously gotten snagged in a Danish structure, in a *faux ami*, closing his eyes to wait alertly for the correct English phrase to float up into his mind, the *mot juste*. Funny, those expressions are all in French—from the time French was the lingua franca.

From time to time he rises from the desk, stretches, does a few push-ups, brews a cup of Nescafé, trying always to have some little translation puzzle in his mind before he does so in order to keep himself rooted in the work.

When he has completed the third page of the article, he glances at the clock and is surprised to see he has worked through lunch time. It is already past one. He eats a ham and cheese and lettuce sandwich standing up in the kitchen, watching the gray sheepdog pace the concrete yard below. Bluett taps on the window, but the dog does not look up. Snubbed by a dog. Then he drinks a glass of water, brushes his teeth, and goes back to his desk.

For a moment before he starts back to work, the thought of the box flitters across his mind. He ignores it, plunges back into the text.

He compels himself to do six pages, to prove to himself that he is in control, and when he is done, well into the second article, it is just past four. He stacks the pages he has worked on and corrected in red ink. Tomorrow he will key in the corrections, do another five pages. He has nothing to complain about. He thinks about taking a drink before going down to the basement, stands before the shelf of bottles in the kitchen, considering.

There is a knock at the door. The sound startles him, jerks him into a near crouch there in the kitchen as he considers not answering, pretending he is not home. *Should install a peep hole.* Another tap.

Nonsense.

He opens the door and sees his daughter's smiling face.

"Raffaella!"

Unalloyed pleasure sweeps his heart as he hugs her, touches her cheek with his lips, cool and fresh with winter, looks at her again, tall and bright-faced, long auburn hair draping the shoulders of a long camel coat. He hears distant music, notes she is wearing earphones—the Discman he gave her for Christmas.

"What are you listening to?"

She plucks one bud from her ear and puts it to his. He hears a low voice burbling words in a slurred growl, hears the words *disease . . . infect me . . . reject me . . . don't want to exist.* He frowns amicably.

"Bad Religion," she says. "They're really tough. You could borrow it if you want. Could I get my Arab on Radar back?"

"Noise Rock," he says and steps back to let her in, watching with pleasure how she acts as if it is her own place, hanging her coat on the wall hooks in the little foyer, going to the kitchen for a Coke from the refrigerator that she knows he stocks for her. "Got any potato chips?"

"On the counter there."

She glances out the back window. "Oh, look, Dad! That dog is so *cute!* Aw, look, he's all lonely and sad out there alone by himself. Look, he's so lonely he wants to go in! How can they do that to him?"

Bluett slips the CD she'd left him into her coat pocket, puts on Coltrane, selects "Central Park West," pours himself a vodka while she turns on the television, surfs to MTV, and he comes back and douses Coltrane while some big black dude wearing an unbuttoned vest and no shirt raps.

She looks at him as if she has just remembered something, although he can see it has been at the front of her mind all along and knows right away what it is, cautions himself not to make an issue of it as he once foolishly did with his son, causing embarrassment and pain over nothing, over peanuts.

"Oh, Dad, uh, before I forget, do you think you could lend me a little bit till next week?"

He nods, averting his eyes. Somehow that she also asks for money makes him less concerned that his son had, too. Of course they ask for money. They need help. Kids need help. "How much you need?"

Her expression is braced for a reaction. "Two hundred?"

He takes out his wallet, lifts out two hundred-kroner bills, then peels off a third, same as he gave Tim, no favorites here, feels relieved it wasn't more. "I just got some money," he lies. "So it's no problem." He remembers how his mother, after his father died, used to give him money without complaint. Still it makes him feel insecure. Would they come and visit anyway? His mother always used to say, *I don't want any duty visits.* He chides himself for his thoughts, looks with pleasure at the girl. He is so proud to be her father, to be the father of two fine, smart, good-looking kids. They are the only worthwhile product of his ungodly life.

"Boy, are you good-lookin', El!"

She beams; her cheekbones glow. High school turned out to be a good thing for her, and he is so grateful for that, that her life has gotten so much better. She hadn't so many friends in grade school and the teachers didn't recognize her. Either she was invisible or she was teased, perceived as being overweight, but she wasn't overweight, she was just a big girl. At a parent-teacher meeting once, one of the teachers, explaining to Bluett and his wife why she hadn't given Raffaella a higher grade, had said, "Well, I think we can all agree, Raffaella is, well, *heavy.*"

"*Heavy?*"

"Yes, you know, heavy and . . . *slow.*"

"She's not in the least slow. Have you ever seen her on *horseback*? She's quick and intelligent, and physically she's agile and strong." He had looked at the teacher's face, a scrawny, wrinkled face with protruding eyes, and a little smile on her thin lips and in her eyes that said, *Nothing enters here.*

But the summer after grade school, Raffaella grew several inches, and then in high school, the kids sought her out, even her grades improved. Now she was at the university studying philosophy.

"So what's new, honey? How's life? Still riding?"

"I couldn't get the hour I wanted so I'm skipping this season."

He nods, hiding his relief, his fear of her being flipped, hurt, paralyzed. She has been riding since she was eight, had plagued them for permission to since she was five.

"How about your piano lessons?"

She drinks from her Coke glass, puts it down on the table, nodding. "It's combined with song now. I really love it."

"That's great, El." He thinks about his own high school and college years. They were happy, too, on the surface at least, except when his father died. He used to hide his grief. He wonders if she is hiding hers. He wants to ask if she's happy, but the question sounds so ridiculous, *is* ridiculous. *What would you answer yourself if she asked you that? I get by. We get by.*

"Little El," he says.

"Dad." Her tone warns him not to be sentimental, even though he can see she likes it a little, likes to have it and protest both.

"How's Jens-Martin? He treating you right?"

"He's okay."

Bluett thinks of the boy, whom he has met only twice, briefly, thinks of his little girl living with him. That's how it is now. The two of them in a little two-room walk-up. No bath. They have to wash at the kitchen sink. Still. Must be nice for them. Better than the hysteria of his generation, constantly hunting, lonely and hoping, hunting, yearning for the touch of another human being.

"Why don't the two of you come over here sometime? Say hi. I'll take you out to dinner, around the corner at that good Eyetalian joint."

"That would be nice."

"Just say the word."

"I'll have to talk to Jens-Martin."

"How's he doing at school?"

"Fine."

"Halfway through, isn't he?"

She nods, lifts her glass again. "Two years left."

Bluett sips his vodka, thinks about Jens-Martin, who doesn't speak much when they meet, who thinks he is a writer. Bluett feels skepticism rise inside himself, vetoes it. Maybe he really *is* a writer. Maybe he's good. He wishes he could get more information from his daughter, wishes the words, the emotions would just flow out, that he could *know* how she is doing. He thinks of Sam's boy, wonders if El would like him.

"Remember Sam?" he says. "Across the hall? My friend? He died."

Her gray eyes grow large. "What happened?"

A pause. Then he decides. "Cancer."

How distant death must seem to a kid, he thinks. Her life has not yet been touched by it. He fills his mouth with chill vodka, swallows. "How was your party last week, your homecoming party there at the school?"

Her smile vanishes. "It was lousy. A bunch of bums showed up, and they ruined everything. Remember Hanne Louise? I was in the hall, going out with her to the toilets, and these four guys were there blocking the stairs, and they said I could pass 'cause I was tough, but this ugly kid with pimple scars all over his face said to Hanne, 'But you're ugly, bitch, you should die,' and he shoved her down the stairs. Just like that."

"My God, what happened, what did you do? Where was Jens-Martin? You should have got the principal to call the cops."

"Jens-Martin didn't come." She laughs a little at herself. "I went crazy. I started yelling at them, scolding them . . ."

"Ella, Ella, you have to be careful . . ."

"They didn't know what to do. They just left."

He laughs then, thinks about how gutsy she's always been, how when she was just a little tiny kid she would crawl up onto the back of a horse that stood higher than Bluett's head. But he thinks of those guys at Christiania, of what might have happened to her. "You were lucky," he says. "Don't try that number again, your luck might run out. How about Hanne Louise? She come over it okay?"

El's face clouds again. "She sprained her ankle a little and had a couple of bruises, but it's not just that. How would it make a person feel to be told they're ugly and get shoved down the stairs for it, that you should *die* for it? There was another kid there who threatened one of the boys with a knife. And Mr. Jensen, the principal? He didn't do a thing. He wouldn't even call the police. He said it would be bad for the school's reputation and would ruin the party for the others."

"That *ass*! That pompous *ass*! I should have known better than to send you to a Catholic school. Notorious goddamn cowards." He takes a breath, waits for his anger to pass. "I'm proud of you, Ella, but please don't take a chance like that again. Please. You were lucky, but the kids today, some of them are nasty. Everything is so crazy. Please take care of yourself, honey. You're the best I have. You and Timothy. You're my treasures. You got to make it through."

"*Yeah*, Dad," she drawls. "Yeah, yeah."

Through to what?, he's thinking afterward, after she has rinsed out her Coke glass and turned off the TV, repositioned her earphones, put the three hundred-crown notes in her wallet, slipped on her coat, and hugged him, the smell of winter in her camel coat, and he watches her descend the stairs, then goes to the window and opens it and calls good-bye, and she turns and waves, and he watches the back of her coat disappear along the street. His little girl.

He cools his forehead against the white window frame, hears himself think, *Please God, protect her and Tim*, watches himself there, praying, feels the skepticism rise up, but at the same time recognizes there is a point at which there is nothing else but to beg the mercy of some power and order beyond one's ken. He wonders if there are people who never get to that, if it is simply his background, the Catholic childhood, that brings him back to it when there is nothing else. But there must be *something*. Otherwise there is nothing. And how could these intricate organisms have developed from *nothing*? There has to be *something*. Far far beyond his ken, but still . . .

He remembers how his father used to say to him, *You've got to have faith in the old man upstairs, son.*

"The old man." *PC would come and get you for that today, Dad. Or is god or God still a man?* He considers the fact that the foundations of his own life seem so insubstantial compared to those of his parents—or what he had imagined, assumed to be, those of his parents. Why had they not managed to extend that foundation to him? Or why had he not managed to receive it? What had they given him at all?

They did teach him some things, some good things. They tried to teach him to be kind, the value of caring about others' feelings. They taught him to think, to value books. They wanted him to believe in God the way they did, in religion, but somehow it all broke down, and when he moved away from it, they didn't question his decision. It seemed to him they had come from such a sound background, the sea of faith still at its full, and had delivered him to the time of the melancholy long withdrawing roar, had sent him off into such a broken future, over which of course they had no control. None of it held up, not God, not country, not family. There was more here for him, in Denmark, where at least people felt responsible to build a social system that provided for everybody—health care, education, basic needs. If that doesn't go broke and collapse.

Still he missed his own country, his own people. He *had* to stay here now, for his health care, his pension. His children were here; what did he have other than his children? And really he loves it here. He could not live in the U.S. again.

He does not feel bitter or disappointed, really. Life has its compensations. It is a joy merely to drink the air and feel the sun. To walk on human legs and look at the sky and the lake and the young healthy bodies of one's children. Their faces cracking open in a smile, their jokes and laughter, their requests for money, anything. He only wishes he had something more to give them, a real legacy, something to build a life on that had a past and a present and a future that were one. Maybe it is up to *them* to make that future. And he wonders then what future he himself had made for himself.

He remembers once, years earlier, reading in an interview with some poet—Jack Gilbert—who said something like, "I'm happy. You have to be happy. God requires it." And the interviewer had said, "So you believe in God," and the poet had said, "No. But I feel so grateful."

12. Equinox

What then?

Another day, another five pages, another evening, another vodka. Coltrane. Chair at the window watching the blue hour descend like a mist. McCoy Tyner's quiet piano chords lead into Coltrane's moody tenor, addressing the equinox. Ought to get some skates, glide like a shadow over the blue ice, hearing music recorded nearly forty years earlier; himself just a tiny lad, his parents young and good-looking. He has "Equinox" on repeat, vodka on his tongue; the tenor enters his ears like a sweet promise, orders his mind with sound that is a credible reality.

He sets down his drink, closes his eyes, sways in his chair, moving to echoes cut into wax a handful of decades earlier. Sweet Jesus, he murmurs, smiling, this is the sound for a lonely hour. If the pope had any sense at all he would canonize this man who works miracles of illumination in the souls of the dead.

Bluett drinks again, studies Steve Davis's bass, Elvin Jones's stick work, as the tenor stays cool, moving out to the last notes of Tyner's ivory.

Then it is over and he cannot bear to hear it again, reaches to poke the stop key and sits in the silence, the lake now steeped in dusk.

He misses Sam at this moment. How many days since he departed? He will be departed forever now. For whatever of forever remains for him. How good it might be to smoke some weed with him, hear some sides, talk. He thinks of Sam alone across the hall the night he did it, drinking half a bottle of booze, swallowing pills, putting the bag over his head, the tie around his wrists. Bluett had checked the stereo but it was empty. He went off without music. Down so low he didn't even care to have any sounds lead him out. Or maybe afraid music would break his resolve to go through with it. Down to Black Dam Lake. A man who yearns for music has a reason to go on.

He peers out into the dark over the frozen lake and sees or thinks he sees a shape there, a smoke-black, man-sized pillar of cloud upright on the ice, and at the same moment an acrid smell rises up his throat into his nose. He shudders. It is as if the cloud pillar addresses him, standing majestically, demanding.

Bluett coughs and the acrid stench now fills his nose and throat with burning. He coughs, swallows more vodka. There is nothing. Nothing on the ice. Nothing in his nose. But a thought in his mind.

The box.

He has been putting it off all week. Afraid of what he might find. Or not find.

After many moments he rises, fixes the door so it won't lock and descends the stairs into the basement, feeling along the damp wall for a light switch.

The concrete floor is wet; the lake seeps up through breaks in the concrete and gathers until the pump sucks it up and spits it down the drain. A puddle splashes against the sole of his shoe. He mutters, opens the door to his storage space and waves in the air for the string switch, stands scanning all his cartons of junk there. Old financial records. Family photos. Letters. Books. Old clothing he could not quite bring himself to throw out. Junk. He ought to burn the lot so his kids never have to confront this gloomy pile of trash, hoping perhaps to discover some clue, some answer, and rooting through to find nothing but worthless junk.

Shoved back beneath a splintery raw-wood shelf, on top of one of his large packing crates, is a brown cardboard carton the size of a large cake box, sealed with heavy duct tape. Printed in marking ink on top are the letters SF, and c/o P. BLUETT. The box is light in his hands, and he stands there wondering again what his instructions were from Sam. He cannot quite recall the conversation. He could take this right now and shove it into the trash barrel outside. The garbage men would come on Monday and cart it away, burn it, and that would be the end of it. He knows he will find nothing of consequence here, no answers, he feels sure of that. Let a man's secrets die with him.

Yet Sam had taken the trouble to ask to leave it here, had left it here, had not wanted to burn it before taking his life. If he had not wanted someone to see it, he would have burned it himself.

Bluett carries the box up to his apartment, steps out of his damp-soled shoes at the door, not to dirty the carpet with the lake water he has stepped in, and puts the box on the oak table.

For some time, he stands there, staring at the box. Then he sits on the sofa and watches it from across the room before going to the kitchen for a steak knife, which he plunges into the seam at the center of the lid, tracing the blade across and around the edges of the flaps.

He finds himself wondering for a moment if Sam was murdered, dismisses the thought as melodramatic nonsense. There had been no question from the police. *Sam killed himself. The note explained it. That was it. So what could be here in this box that is any business of yours?*

The box is a mess of paper. Credit card receipts, some legal documents, notebooks, business letters, financial papers, a few photographs. One of the photos is of the Russian woman, Svetlana Krylova, wearing black stockings and a black leather corset. Her chin is tilted, a small arrogant smile on her lips. The other pictures are of Sam in a tuxedo, of Sam's son and daughters as children, some others of ordinary-looking people Bluett does not know.

Bluett studies the one of Svetlana Krylova, puts it aside, shuffles through the papers. There are final statements from a canceled bank account. He runs his finger up the column, following a reverse growth from three hundred thousand crowns up through zero. More than fifty thousand dollars. The withdrawals are large, nothing less than ten thousand crowns, a few of twenty-five thousand, and the last two of fifty thousand crowns each. He puts the statements aside, next to the photo of Svetlana Krylova, continues to sort through the papers.

He comes to a credit card receipt from the Satin Club for nine thousand crowns, another for five thousand, another for eighty-five hundred. There are more, over a course of three or four months, perhaps twenty of them. He goes to his desk for a large envelope, stuffs in the receipts and the bank statements, the photograph, and sits wondering what it is he hopes to do with them, what they mean.

Maybe Sam made a fool of himself and killed himself in shame. Maybe he had cancer and wanted a last fling before he went out. Maybe something else. He thinks of the photograph, the smile, the leather.

He turns back to the box and dumps the rest of it on the table. In a large envelope, he finds a letter from a lawyer on Købmagergade, noting that Sam's apartment has been sold to Ms. Svetlana Krylova, that his insurance, pension plan, and savings will be divided equally between his children. The savings account number is given; it matches the number on the canceled account, the one that has been drained to nothing. The insurance, Bluett guesses, will be canceled out by the suicide. *At least they got the pension plan*, he thinks and looks to see how much that is. It is a capital pension, but he sees that that too has been drawn on, borrowed against. What remains is insignificant—a few thousand to each kid, not even the forty thousand the estate agent had estimated. Where did the rest go? He looks at the photo of Svetlana again, the arrogant smile. The letter from the lawyer shows a carbon copy to Ms. Svetlana Krylova, which seems odd to Bluett, as if Sam were trying to prove something to her. That he loved her? Or something else?

Out the window, all the many windows of the buildings across the lake reflect their squares of yellow light in the black surface of the ice. He thinks of all the people rumored to have taken their lives in the lake, thinks of those reflections as windows to their watery graves, thinks of the lake water seeping up through the earth into the basement of this building.

His breath is shallow. He looks at the phone, thinks of friends, acquaintances he might call. A woman he knows in Norway whom he feels very close to, who has a clear mind, but what would her husband think to have him calling her like that, and what would he say? Cry out for comfort? Words? Advice? Whimper? Whine? Say, *Ain't life a bitch, sweetheart?*

There was a cousin in New York he knew would be happy to hear his voice, a friend in San Diego who would sense his need and try to buddy him through, another in Chicago. There was his sister, of course, but she had so many worries of her own. There were two or three friends here in Copenhagen, but what would he say to them, and what would it change?

What he could say was that he had seen Sam's eyes the day he died, that he had their startled blue gaze imprinted in his soul, the gaze of a man who knew he was going to his death, who was not saying good-bye so much as gazing across the threshhold at him, nothing left to say, nothing left.

He puts on Coltrane, "Equinox" again, and goes for the vodka, returns with it to the oak table and the pile of papers with Coltrane's tenor in his head. He stuffs the legal papers into his envelope. *Sam's "dossier,"* he thinks. *For what?*

Most of the rest he sifts through seems to be without significance, and he drops it, piece by piece, back into the cardboard box for possible later review. Near the bottom of the pile he finds a sheaf of folded yellow legal pages covered with handwriting. The handwriting is scrawled across them, perpendicular to the lines, like words behind bars. He recognizes the handwriting as Sam's.

On the first page is a title that has been scratched out, and beneath the scribble he can just make out the word *memoir*, also lined out repeatedly. The next page is blank and the next begins, "There is a life inside me I have never revealed to others, maybe not even myself in a way. Memories I treasure. Reflections of strange passion."

Or perhaps it says "*strong* passion." Bluett cannot see for sure.

I do not understand these feelings and never have but I only know that they are connected to something in me very powerful, a feeling of what I expect religious people mean by the word *grace* even if what causes that feeling are events far from what I would connect with religious things or prayers or whatever else. It is not always an event. Sometimes it is a reaction to an event. I can remember certain things vividly and some-times they are only a glimpse of something.

For example, Helene Graham in fourth grade meeting my eye with a secret, excited smile when the nun smacked me in front of the class for some-thing I didn't do. Why should that memory be one of my treasures? I have relived it a thousand, ten thousand times in the years since. Helene Graham lives in my heart because of that smile of pleasure at my humiliation.

To think of cruelty to children is so ugly to me but the memory of Helene enjoying my humiliation is a treasure. I see her face, and her freckles; and her thin lips that resembled the color of a raspberry, her blue eyes full of sparkles.

And now I am fifty-five years old and all of my life this and other similar things have lived onward as secrets in me that I have always feared to explore—

Or perhaps it says "feared to explain."

Even when it was offered to me I turned away from it, unable to reveal this part of me, so fearful of how ridiculous and pitiful, contemptible I might seem to those few people whose opinion of me I valued and value if they ever found out.

Can't a man have another life? Shall one live with unfulfilled longing forever?

I do not wish to be the subject of my own morbid self-absorption, but there are experiences I long for as a person longs for grace and it seems so futile to be forever in control.

There are men who go to prostitutes for this, but that is commerce and as far from what I am looking for as anything could be, yet I know that if this ever were exposed it would destroy me, I could not live it down.

The journal goes on in this vein for several pages, occasionally giving an account of a memory or perhaps a fantasy, mostly brief instants that apparently captured his mind or soul with passion. There is an account of an evening at scout camp around a fireplace in a cabin where one boy is made to answer twenty questions, for each of which he cannot answer he is to remove one article of clothing. Sam describes a fever rising in the room as the boy fails again and again and is left wearing only his underpants, standing in front of the fire, and the last question is posed, and he is unable to answer.

We all jumped to our feet. I was with them even if I hated myself for taking part in Serenies's humiliation. He was so clearly miserable with the situation, but unable to get himself out of it and therefore so much the victim. So abandoned to his own victimhood that it seemed like he was ordained for it, and as he stood there in the firelight looking at the eager hungry faces around him in the dark he was pretty as a girl. He trembled and begged with his eyes, and I wanted to free him if I could, but I couldn't, and even as I was caught by my own desire to see his complete exposure and humiliation, I was afraid of what might happen to him when he was completely naked. There was so much heat in the room, and I wished I could help him but then I understood that more than that what I wished and wish for was to be him, to be in his position, to be the one standing in the firelight almost naked while all those faces stared hungry at me for my exposure.

Bluett puts the diary aside and sits back in his chair, listens again to Coltrane play "Central Park West," mellow bittersweet lines of music full of longing for human love so pure and so sad. He sips his vodka and glances at the pages on the table before him. He does not want to read more, but he knows he will read it all. The pages tremble in his fingers, and he feels a dropping deep in his stomach that is a mix of embarrassment and sympathy for Sam.

There are half a dozen similar entries of events spaced out through Sam's life, always producing a passion, a desire so powerful he did not dare to respond to it, frozen by the power of its attraction.

Is it evil? Or is it grace? It feels like grace. It feels like something holy. Or is it the flame that kills the moth? I believe that many men, maybe all men, have a shadow life, and that most men hide it and that that is why they are so willing to attack one whose secrets are revealed and why it is necessary to keep them hidden. I know this from bitter experience.

He then went on to tell a story of his one attempt to try to bring his desires into reality. He was seventeen years old, living in a small town in northern California. One of his friends had told him about a woman who lived in a trailer on the other side of town and who did strange things for money. He questioned the boy about these strange things and received sketchy details, but enough to make him understand.

By asking indirect questions, studying the map, taking exploratory night drives, he finally located the woman's trailer. He drove by frequently, and always there was a car parked outside, often different cars. Sometimes he saw an automobile pull up, a man step out, look over his shoulder, go in. Once he waited and saw the man come out again, walking slowly, limping. He copied the name from the mailbox, looked in the local phone book, got a number and called, and a woman's voice answered.

He was afraid to go to her because he had once seen a police car parked outside, afraid he might be arrested, so the woman agreed to come with him, to follow him in her car to a place she knew in the woods where they would be undisturbed.

It cost a lot of money, a large part of the savings from his high school job, but the experience fulfilled his greatest dreams, an experience of profound beauty, despite the strangeness of it. It was dusk in the woods, a balmy summer night. She dressed him as a woman, in the clothes he had brought with him, then she went through the question game with him, and when he had come to the end of it, she did other things that they had discussed in advance. He had been unable to find release so when she left him he put on the women's underclothes and stockings and sat in the backseat of his car to masturbate.

That was how the police found him. They brought him in and would not allow him to put on his own clothes again. They put him in a cell like that, with three other men, and phoned his father to come and get him. His father was most upset about the fact that the clothes he had taken were his sister's. "How could you have put on your own sister's clothes for such a purpose?" he asked him again and again.

He was charged with violation of a state penal code against public lewdness and "unnatural sexual acts" and because he was not yet eighteen years old, it was up to the judge whether or not to release his name and details of his arrest to the local press. The judge decided to do so. The story was printed in the newspaper, along with his name and address.

There had been nothing for him to do then but leave town, to start a new life somewhere. He had an uncle in England who took him in and eventually he made his way to Denmark, where he met his wife to be. On the night she accepted his proposal of marriage, Sam told her that he had once gone to jail, that he had been convicted of a crime in California, that he would prefer not to tell her what it was, but if she wished him to, he would do it. She told him she did not want him to tell her anything that would make him unhappy, and they left it at that.

A dozen years later, after their children had been born, she woke him in the middle of the night and said that she could not stand it any longer. He would have to tell her. All those years it had been preying on her and now, when they had children, her not knowing what it might be was too much for her, she could no longer bear it. Had he raped a child? Killed? What?

He told her.

At first she laughed, but with a strange light in her eye that she then turned on him, and he could see repugnance in her eyes. He tried to talk it through with her. She assured him it was nothing, it was insignificant, people were free to have their desires, but finally, after he had pursued it for some weeks, she admitted that it would have been easier for her to accept if it had been murder. This was so . . . ludicrous. She had lost respect for him. Especially when he admitted that he still had these desires, that he had been keeping them hidden from her all those years.

"Do you put on my things?" she asked him, and he saw such revulsion in her eyes, heard it in her voice, that he saw he must bury it all away again.

He quickly assured her that it was no longer the same. He lied to her, said that she had misunderstood, he no longer desired any of it. He could only remember the desire from the confusion of his youth. He thought that she halfway believed the lies, that she wanted to believe them, but he could see that it was the end of intimacy for them. She never looked at him again without a trace of that expression in her eyes being visible to him. Or did he project it? No, it was there.

He knew then that he could never reveal this to another person. He could not bear the thought of being looked at with such revulsion.

Until he and his wife had parted and he met Svetlana.

The journal ends there, gives no account of his time with Svetlana.

Bluett sits back. The Coltrane has ended, and it is so dark outside that all he can see from where he sits is his own reflection in the black glass. He glances to the walls, the masks there, the one with the corkscrew eyes drawing him in. He has refilled his glass several times as he read the journal, and he can feel the vodka in him, in the heaviness of his chest, the flatness of his mind.

His eyes roam the apartment, taking in the film of dust on the television, the stereo, crumbs on the coffee table, scattered beneath. He tries but cannot remember the last time he cleaned, then realizes it was not so long ago, when Liselotte was coming. He stares at the African phallus on the wall and remembers the games he played with her and wonders what they meant, what they were after, trying to fill each other's emptiness.

What *had* they been after?

Whatever it was, he thinks, it was not treachery. Fumbling perhaps, misunderstanding, but not fucking treachery.

13. Like Paradise

He dreams that he is not asleep, but lying awake in bed with the light on working through intricate thought patterns. At some point, he reaches a conclusion so startling that he wakes, sits up and gropes at the night stand for a pen to write it down, realizes that the light is not on, hits the lamp switch, gets his glasses on and sits there on the edge of the bed with a ballpoint and pad, but his mind is empty.

He can remember nothing of his sleeping thoughts. Yes, he recalls meeting his father in a dream sleep. He called to him, "Dad! Dad!" and his father turned, winked.

"Know what I'm doing now, son? I'm the ambassador." He smiled. "See you at the embassy, son, eh?"

He staggers out to the bathroom, pees, rinses his vodka-parched mouth, crawls back under the feather blanket and sinks like a stone, wakes to the eight-o'clock church bell with throbbing temples and his heart full of hatred for the arrogant smile of the thieving bitch who has cheated Sam's children of their modest inheritance. It is clear to him now what she has done, how she has played him, no doubt teased out of him all the information in his diary, his fear, his vulnerability.

It occurs to him then that it is Saturday. No pages today. He rises, pulls on old jeans and a sweatshirt, gets out the vacuum cleaner from the hall closet, attaches the aluminum pipes and runs the carpet-sweeper attachment over the rug beneath the dining table, coffee table, the TV stand.

In the bedroom, he vacuums beneath the desk and shelving, pulls out the sofa bed and sees something white stuck in against the wall. Liselotte's bra. He puts it to his face, inhaling, feels hot and lonely and yearns for her.

Then he gets mad at her again, kicks the on button for the vacuum and starts running it over the carpet again.

He chucks his dirty clothes into a plastic basket, carries it down to the basement, and stuffs the clothes into the washer, pours in soap, adjusts the temperature, the spin, waits to hear the water begin to pipe in, standing in the puddles of lake water that have seeped up through the floor.

Upstairs, he kicks off his damp shoes, fills a red plastic bucket with hot water and Ajax and scours the tub and shower stall, the bathroom sink, the chrome faucets. He gets into the slots of the gunky drain with alcohol-dipped Q-tips, pokes into each hole, swabs. The mirror he takes with Windex and a piece of dry, torn T-shirt, swipes away the toothpaste spatters, finger smudges. On his knees, he cleans the tile floor with a rag.

He empties the dirty bucket water into the toilet, flushes, refills the bucket and takes on the woodwork in the living room, the coffee table, the TV, stereo, window ledges, watching the grime come away on his rag, which he dips into the bucket, rings, dips again and wipes across an end table, seeing the film of dust disappear in swipes—just like a TV commercial.

He attacks the kitchen sink with a scouring pad, turns to the countertops, the linoleum. At last he scours the toilet, flushes, scours again, pours Drano in the sink and runs the hot water until the sink water empties smoothly.

Downstairs again, he shifts the wet laundry to the dryer and sets it for forty-five minutes, comes back up to wash his hands and drink a cup of Nescafé at the window.

Across the lake he sees a fox dash out of the bushes, run along the bank in the sunlight, and disappear again through a stand of trees.

Liselotte's bra is on the oak table. He takes it in his fingers, feeling the soft, cool material against his skin, sighs, goes in to shower, scrubs his scalp, his skin, his neck, the soles of his feet, stands for a long time beneath the hot spray, letting it beat against his head and wash down over his body.

By late afternoon, he stands at the window in a clean shirt, silk tie, slacks, jacket, sipping his first vodka of the day as the yolk-gold sunlight burns across the ice of the lake.

He slips on his Burberry trenchcoat and takes a long walk around the lakes, turning right to the near end and across to the Black Dam Embankment, which he follows all the way into the western side of the city. He wears clip-on shades against the sunset and walks at a fast pace along the outer edge of Copenhagen's old city, where the lepers once lived and no one else. He thinks now of the expanses of dwellings running all the way up north to Helsingør and beyond, thinks of Hamlet's castle there. Revenge. Failed revenge. The failed righting of a wrong. *Shakespeare must have known Denmark*, he thinks. *Denmark in winter, a landscape of brooding doubt.*

He feels good, legs taking long strides, arms swinging, breath easy, steaming from his nostrils. Without breaking stride, he threads around a girl on a rattling bicycle, steps to the side for a couple with a stroller.

He crosses the Peace Bridge, past the Café Front Page, past the little boat dock, crosses Queen Louise's Bridge, and walks the embankment of Peblinge Lake, trying to remember some tale he read about this lake, about an aristocrat thrown into the water by three drunken soldiers. Did he drown? Was his spirit still trapped there in the water, spirit of vengeance?

Ducks paddle toward him as he approaches, a patch circling out from the bank where the authorities have melted the ice to accommodate the birds; they think he has come to feed them as so many do, throwing them the rest of the bread from their lunches.

A white swan, wings arched gracefully behind it, glides along the golden black water. Overhead he hears an eerie yet familiar whirring sound, looks up to see four swans in flight, long necks stretched out flat before them, wings flapping in unison.

He once knew a woman who was walking her dog along the embankment. She removed the leash so it could run free, a little French terrier, and the dog jumped into the lake for a swim. A swan glided over and with one sweep of its neck broke the dog's spine, then held it under until it had drowned. Bluett always thinks of this story when he sees a representation of the five flying swans that symbolize the five Nordic countries. A swan appears elegant and peaceful, but it is fierce as an eagle.

The sun hangs low now behind the white Lake Pavilion, a building that looks like some Walt Disney representation of fantasy land. He crosses Gyldenløvsgade to the so-called Svineryggen, Swine Back Path, which runs along the last of the lakes, Saint George's—named for the patron saint of lepers, here where the leper colony stood several hundred years earlier, outside the gates of the city. He thinks about this as he walks, the fate of the lepers, fate, what happens to all of us, each of us.

He crosses Kampmannsgade Bridge and takes the last link of Saint George's Lake, still on Swine Back, down to Gammel Kongevej, where he turns left under the foot of the lakes and heads in toward the city. He knows where he is going, but there is no hurry.

How cold the city grows in the dark, the eerie sweeps of green in the night sky, red stains of neon, Saturday nightlife beginning to stir on the chill pavements.

He glances surreptitiously at people passing by, wonders about their lives, especially the lives of these people, out on the street at a time when the great family Denmark is sitting down to dinner, perhaps with guests, just slicing the edge of a spoon into a halved avocado filled with tiny fjord shrimp, taking a discreet mouthful while they wait for the host or hostess to raise a glass, say *skål*. All glasses lift, eyes meet, lips sip, the glasses are presented again, the eating resumes. The cozy visits. Who are they to one another? This is a question Bluett has never solved for himself, not in twenty years of living the Danish family life with his wife and in-laws. What do they mean to one another? They seem so cool, so distant, yet perhaps that is only because he is a foreigner among them, could speak Danish with them but perhaps not quite well enough.

All their rituals—the three days of Christmas, joining hands to circle the tree and sing together gazing up at the candles burning on the tree, the Easter lunches in the country, the Advent Sunday gatherings, burning the straw witch on midsummer night—year after year of ritual gatherings with those of your blood, and still he asks himself what they *are* to one another. Perhaps it is only that, the mass of ritual, the language, the tradi-tions. And perhaps that is enough. How they love their queen. How so many of these mostly peaceful, tolerant people will turn and hiss like an angry swan if you question their monarchy.

Perhaps it is just the history of their little kingdom—little now, once great, the great times and the broken times, the wars with Germany, Sweden, England, the destruction of their fleet, the loss of northern Germany, of Norway, of southern Sweden, the great fires of this city—a thousand years of history that binds them. Perhaps they do not need to ask what they are to one another. Perhaps it is enough for them to know who they themselves are, who they share their identity with.

But those are the people sitting around their tables now. He wants to know who these people on the street are: foreigners like himself, even if only in spirit? What are they out looking for? What do they hope might wait for them in the night? Young men, of course, are seeking young women, and young women young men. Other men of course seek men or boys, and other women seek women, and yet others seek other things. They are not all young. And what are they seeking? Those not going to the theater, to the movies, those only walking the cold dark streets?

He has worked up a sweat walking, and his feet are chilled, his mouth dry, belly empty. He goes into a steak house by the Town Hall Square, Hereford Beefstouw, and is shown to a table by a smiling blonde waitress. He slips off his Burberry, and the waitress smiles at him as though she cares deeply for his welfare and asks if he would like to start with a drink, and while he waits for his vodka, blows his nose and warms the frosted lenses of his glasses, he knows that for the time it takes him to eat, to drink his vodka and his wine, he has a purpose, he has a place to be, an appetite to still, and the loneliness will stay outside on the cold dark streets. He has his hour in this warmth, yet knowing it is but an hour, even two if he stretches it with dessert, coffee, brandy, knowing already that it will end, will end soon, that he will pay the waitress, her smile will fade, he will sling on his coat again, and his full belly will grow heavy as he crosses the restaurant floor to the door, steps out again into the night with nothing, nowhere, nobody awaiting him.

He thinks perhaps this is why people hold together a broken marriage for as long as they can, the sense of *this* waiting for them outside, the sense of this and the fear they will only do the same thing again anyway, make the same mistake, end in the same ill-understood trap framed by their own ill-understood character. *You must want to be alone,* he says to himself. *You do. You always did. You must have.*

An image of Liselotte rises into his thoughts, her smiling face, her warm gaze on him, her sparkling amber eyes. Is it really hopeless? Does it have to be?

The waitress brings his steak and Cabernet and it is perfect.

"I hope it tastes," she says, and he smiles, nods, tips back the last of his vodka. The beef in his mouth is succulent, the Cabernet silky on his tongue. Cheese afterward, Gorgonzola on warm baguette, two radishes and another glass of Cab.

"Dessert?"

"Something light, perhaps."

"We have a delightful fresh sorbet with liqueur."

Coffee. Brandy. Check. Plastic card on the white table cloth. A few crowns extra for service beyond the call, and she is smiling warmly as she helps him on with his trenchcoat, her hand even grazes his shoulder, as though she cannot resist touching him once, cannot bear to let him go without some special tiny intimacy between them. *Orchestration of cynicism*, he thinks. *Or just good business. Good relations.*

The moment always comes.

The door at his back again. The cold night, darker now, streets emptier, for in the meantime the wanderers have gone where they were headed. He stands there now with a scrap of meat between his teeth and does not know what to do with himself until it is time. A bar. But he has to keep his head at least a bit clear. See if any of his old drinking companions are about. At the Palæ, the Bo-Bi, the White Lamb, Rosengaardens Bodega, Charlie's. But anyway, tonight is different. Tonight he has something he must do.

He looks at his watch. Almost time.

Circling around past the parliament, he crosses the Marble Bridge, dodges across through a gap in the traffic flowing out of Amager, and comes up behind the Royal Theater. Just off Kongens Nytorv, he stops outside the door with the brass plate that says

SATIN CLUB

10:00 P.M. TO 4:00 A.M.

RING BELL

His thumb presses the brass button, and he waits. A woman opens the door, smiling skeptically.

"Yes?" she asks.

She is not young, late forties perhaps. She wears a low-cut blouse, but her face is ordinary, the little makeup she wears is tastefully applied.

"May I come in?"

He follows her through a foyer, glimpses a bar through the curtain at the other end. He heads for it.

"Hey?" she calls to him. "It costs two hundred crowns to go in there."

"Can I pay with a card?"

"Of course. Let me take your coat."

The bar is dark and not crowded. A few men sit at tables or on stools around the oval bar, facing the dance floor. Colored lights flash on the floor, and one whole wall is a series of nine large TV screens on which a variety of scenes flicker. He takes a seat at the end of the bar, facing directly onto the abandoned dance floor. Off to the side, he notices three or four women who stand talking near a disco cabin. The woman who let him in is talking to one of them, a younger woman wearing a gray miniskirt and black silk blouse and stockings. Her hair is long and black and her face is beautiful, even-featured, full-lipped, dark-eyed. She is looking respectfully into the face of the older woman speaking to her. She strokes the older woman's arm as she speaks. Then the older woman caresses her cheeks with both her palms, runs one palm along her hip, kisses her lightly on the lips, returns to the bar where Bluett sits.

Apparently she doubles as the barmaid. She serves him a vodka. "Would you like me to hold your card . . ." She looks at the card. ". . . Mr. Bluett?"

"Sure." He wants her to see his name. "Are you the manager?"

She nods.

"Those are very beautiful women."

"Yes, and they are very talented dancers."

"They just dance?"

"It is up to the customers if they want to buy them a drink and talk. If you want to go upstairs and talk, you buy a bottle of champagne, and then you talk. What happens then is between the two of you."

"How much does that cost?"

She glances at him, his tie. Her pale blue eyes chill him despite her easy manner. "The champagne costs one thousand crowns. Then what happens is between you and her. It is a free world. A woman's body is her own to decide upon."

He sips his drink, watches her. There is music playing, Sade, singing about the secrets of the soul, about giving it up, letting it all go, about surrender, surrendering love.

Bluett asks, "Do you have facilities for, uhm, special desires?"

"Of course," she says, and her smile is almost tender beneath the pale blue eyes. "The cellar is also fully equipped with special rooms. Would you like to talk with someone?"

"Not just yet," he says. "I'd really like to see some of the girls dance."

She tells him that Tanya comes on in just a few minutes and points at his glass. A question: Refill? He nods, swivels on the stool just as Prince begins to sing over the sound system, grumbling out words to a background of horns and guitar, and he sees Tanya is the woman in the gray miniskirt. Her clothes are not vulgar but elegant, as are her movements as she dances in the flickering lights, alone on the empty dance floor in the near-empty room. This is just for him.

Bluett fills his mouth with liquor, and Prince sings *sexy mother fucker* as Tanya dances. *Sexy sexy, sexy* . . . Then her blouse is on the floor and he sees a tattoo at the top of her shoulder. She dances near to where he sits, a yard away, watching him as she unhooks her bra and flings it away, dances left, right in front of him, turns away abruptly and presses up against the wall of TV screens, which he begins to notice.

Each screen features a different act or body part, and Tanya's flat outstretched palms glide down those she can reach as she presses up against the wall. On one screen is a naked woman going down on a naked woman, on another a woman going down on a naked man, on yet another a woman in stiletto heels whipping a naked man . . .

Then the dancing woman reaches down and removes her skirt, and there is another tattoo, a flower just above her buttock, and now she dances wearing nothing but one stocking. She dances well, keeping from the borders of vulgarity. Finally she is naked. She rolls on the floor, springs up and, staring full at Bluett, she walks briskly in time to the music across the length of the dance floor toward him, her long black hair swaying across her breasts.

She stops in front of him, not a foot away, staring into his eyes. His breath catches. Her body is flawless, so beautiful, *so fucking sexy*. And what is behind her eyes? In her mind? What is she thinking? Or is she pure instinct, the hypnotist collector? Then she turns her face away and abruptly whips her head so her hair slashes across the distance between them. It lashes his cheek lightly, just as the music ends, and she is retreating without a glance back, gathering her clothes to disappear behind the disco booth.

Bluett turns back to the bar, dry in the mouth. The hostess stands there at a discreet distance, but close enough for contact.

"Some dancer," he says, though he hardly has enough breath to speak. He feels the pressure between his legs as some alien presence.

The manager smiles. "We're lucky to have her. She is one of our best. Shall I ask if she wishes to speak with you?" In her smile he sees that tenderness again, which does not match the glint of power in her eyes.

"No. Thanks. Not yet." He lifts his feet from the rungs of the stool to inflict his will on his body, orders another vodka, trying to think of a way forward that will not be a giveaway. Sade's voice comes on singing about what she can see in the shadow of a man's eyes, and as Bluett sits watching the space beside the disco booth, in the flickering light from the TV screens and the ceiling he sees her there. He recognizes her at once, in the next moment feels doubt, but no, it *is* her, he knows for certain, she is the woman he saw with Sam, the woman who stood on the street beneath Bluett's window the day after Sam died, the woman smiling arrogantly in the photograph in Sam's box of secrets. Svetlana Krylova. With revulsion he feels the pressure returning, understands the power here that undid Sam, that could soften the will, blur boundaries, draw a person through unknown doors.

"Now *she* is beautiful," he says to the hostess. "*She* is beautiful."

"You like? You want to talk to her?"

"I would like that very much."

"She is very special."

"I would love to see her dance."

"She no longer dances out here, but if you wish to talk to her, I will ask for you. It is not any man she will talk to. Or dance for."

Now Sade is singing about surrendering love again, as he watches the hostess cross through the flickering lights past the TV screens, wondering what he will say when Svetlana Krylova comes to him. He trusts he will know. Perhaps he will say nothing, simply talk, pay for her time, see what information he might turn to his use. He doesn't know what he hopes to achieve, whether he can expect to be any match for her, a woman who lives by treachery, a woman with her power. But he wants her to know his name because then she will know he knows what she has done. And where he can find her. And he wants her to know that. Wants her to know he will not forget it. For a short black instant he sees his thumbs at her throat, her eyes captured in the moment before death, realizing it is the end. No. He knows he is incapable of that. Something else. But what? Be still. Watch. Listen.

He sees the hostess by the booth touch Svetlana Krylova's shoulder and speak to her. There is deference in the hostess's posture now, respect. She gestures toward the bar where Bluett sits smiling through the smoky colored lights at them. He can read the sudden tensing of Svetlana Krylova's body, knows he has already been made.

The hostess returns, no sign of uncertainty or reversal in her eyes, on her thin lips. Despite himself, Bluett wonders how it would be with her, realizes how far across the threshold he has come. She steps behind the bar. "She is not available. Would you like to talk to another girl? Tanya?"

"I have a weakness for Russian women."

"Who has said that she is Russian?"

"It's so clear when you got this thing for them."

"Really?" She eyes him. "Well, there is another Russian girl who will dance in a little while . . ."

"I have a weakness for that one."

Her smile now is without even fake tenderness, her eyes unyielding. She takes the glass with his AmEx from the shelf behind her and inserts the card into the slot of the little credit card terminal. "Perhaps you should settle your bill now, Mr. Bluett," she says. Her tone falls at his name, her glance directs his to the disco booth where a tall, thick, bearded man stands looking toward them.

Bluett takes in the size of the man, the hard set of his face, and fear opens in his belly, fear and hatred, but the hatred has nowhere to go, only retreat.

He looks at the check. "First time I ever paid fifty bucks for four centiliters of vodka."

"Our clients do not ask the prize," the woman says. "If you have money troubles, you should have asked about the prizes first."

"You take the prize all right," he says. "You take the bloody biscuit." And draws a line through the gratuity block on the credit card slip, signs it, pockets his card, drains the last of his vodka and melted ice.

Sade is singing again about a love that feels like paradise as he stands by the cloakroom counter and someone he has not seen before, a young blond man with a hard mouth, passes his coat across to him, staring at him.

The lyrics, the echo of the silken voice float through his mind as he steps out into the cold again. *Like paradise.* He buttons his collar to the throat and passes beneath the overhang on the street behind the Royal Theater. Sade's words and the bongos echo in his mind as he walks, and then he hears footsteps from across the street, voices that alert his city caution.

He moves toward the shadow of the wall, looking away, but a bulky man weaves swiftly across the road, calling to him, "Hey, skipper, what time's it? Got the time?" Accented English. Polish?

And Bluett sees the impasse where the wall beside him narrows to a closed angle, and someone is behind him as well.

The bulky man has a blond face. "You got an ugly big fuckin' snotter," he says. "Flatten it for you."

And the fist catches Bluett full on his nose before he even sees it. He groans and falls back against the wall, feels his skull smack the stone as the color and pain of the blow open in his brain and he is on the ground.

"Big-nosed fuckin' Jew, keep your snotter out of other people's business," the voice above him says and a shoe tip thumps hard into his belly. He doubles around it, swinging the flat of his arm in a blow he himself sees as pathetic.

"I'm not even a Jew, you fucking Nazi," he tries to say and hears how meaningless and pointless his words are. His nose, at first numb from the blow, now a sharp arc of pain across his face, his eyes, and another foot lands in the small of his back. Rage flares up in him and instantly fades into surrender, powerlessness. He remembers then advice from somewhere and brings his arms up around his head, curls into a fetal posture, and surrenders with a grunt to the next kick in his back and the next beneath his arm and the next, the next . . .

He loses count, knows only that he is on an icy pavement being kicked. His glasses are gone, and he worries about them for a moment, then he begins to think of his head, wondering if he can keep his brain from damage, whether he will end in a wheelchair, smashed to a street-organ player, as the Danes say. The echo of the expression in his brain almost tricks a smile, but his face hurts very much, the numbness of the blows has opened to pain, and he feels shame at the sound of his voice, through his blood-filled nose, telling which pocket contains his wallet, begging them to take it, but they continue to kick him until one very pointed boot catches him full in the chest and he hears the crack of bone drive a high-pitched scream up through his mouth.

Then the cold and the pain and the humiliation are gone into a fading screen of black-and-white dots, the sounds of footsteps echoing away across the road.

PART IV

Psalm

Tonight Charlie Parker roars on a Harley past himself on the sidewalk
and simultaneously parks a sedan on the Cathedral square
even while he receives the alkies for the evening meal in
the sacristy . . .

—Dan Turèll, "Charlie Parker on Isted Street"

14. A Love Supreme

In the dream he is to climb a steep hill in the great park for an interview with the holy monkey. He trudges up the slick grass slope but is exhausted when he reaches the peak where the monkey waits for him—a tall, skinny, scrawny ape with patchy long hair who cries in tones as shrill as a soprano sax, "Blessed be His name!" Then the monkey looks closely at Bluett, tells him he is too tired for an interview, suggests they nap first and lies down comfortably on the rough earth. Bluett is envious, rolls into an uncomfortable ball, aching against the stony rubble beneath him, but begins to doze off, realizing then he is actually waking up.

To sleep when you're asleep is to wake, he thinks and senses the warning of an approach that opens his eyes in time to see two large hands reaching for his face.

"*Ja, ja,* just so," a man's voice says in Danish as fingers grasp and quickly twist his nose. He hears the crunch of bone in his brain, yells.

"*Præcis,*" the voice says. "Beautiful. *Smukt.*"

He hears the ripping sound of tape and then feels it pressed across the bridge of his nose. He wonders if there is brain damage. The entire front of his head feels as though it has been kicked by a horse.

"That should suffice," the voice says and Bluett opens his eyes to look up into the blurry broad face of a man in a white jacket. "Straight as the proverbial arrow," he says. Bluett turns his head to right and left. He lies bare-chested on a treatment table. He remembers the ambulance then, gingerly reaches to his nose, feels the tape, feels his glasses are missing.

"Why am I here?" he asks. "Where am I?"

"In the trauma center," the doctor says. "You were jumped."

Then he remembers how he lost his glasses, remembers being punched, kicked outside the Satin Club.

The doctor lays one palm flat on Bluett's chest, taps the back of the one hand with the fingers of the other, evoking an involuntary moan from Bluett. He notices now that his ribs are taped on one side.

"*Ja*, it will be tender for a time. Cracked two of them but you'll live, I give you something for the pain tonight, and the nurse at reception will call for a car for you. Or you might get yourself a ride home from the police out there. They want to talk to you."

Bluett breathes in slowly, hears the air snaggle crookedly up his nose and remembers the police on the telephone when he left Christiania, remembers the large, hard-faced man in the Satin Club and that sense of his own powerlessness, and he knows the police can do nothing to help him now, feels somehow they will want him to release them, to validate their pointless bureaucracy that helps nothing. He feels they will try to make him say things that are not true in order to be free of this obstacle to the remainder of their shift. "I don't want to talk to them."

"That sounds suspicious," says another voice from behind the doctor, and Bluett narrows his eyes to try to see. Two blurs stand in the doorway. He tightens the squint and sees uniforms.

"You reasonably drunk, are you?" the shorter blur asks.

"I was jumped." He hears the thickness of his own voice, feels it in the throbbing of his nose, and he has no plan for what he will say, how much of it he will give them. "It was them. At the Satin Club. Outside. Svetlana Krylova."

"You were jumped by someone called Svetlana Krylova?" asks the taller one. "A woman did this to you?"

"I was jumped after I left the Satin Club. After I asked for Svetlana Krylova."

"Who is Svetlana Krylova?"

Bluett thinks, tries to think, waits for his mind to tell him something to say. "Who?" he says. "I don't know. Maybe it was the Russian mafia. Or the bikers. Like at Christiania."

"You were at Christiania, too? You on something? You smoke some hash maybe?"

"That was before."

"You were on something before?"

"I was at Christiania before. Days ago, a week. I've just been kicked in the head. I can't remember. It has nothing to do with this. Last week. But I saw someone beat up and called you guys and you wouldn't come."

The doctor says, "I think it is difficult for him to be talking just now."

"You have so much money to piss away at the Satin Club?" the shorter policeman says.

The pain is localized in two blunt vertical lines at the center of the brain behind Bluett's forehead, where an image remains of the tall, skinny, scrawny ape with patchy long hair, crying shrilly and musically, "Blessed be His name!" Somehow the words are comforting, although he feels very sorry for himself and tries to reason through this moment, to master the emotion that threatens to squeeze tears from his eyes. "Are we playing blame the victim here, then? Remember me? I'm the guy who got beat up and kicked around," he says and hears a whimper in his voice.

"What were you doing in the Satin Club?"

"We never got any complaints from the Satin Club," the other policeman says. "Never any complaints."

Bluett thinks, *That must be because they pay you pretty good.* Then he thinks for some time about what he was doing in the Satin Club, tries to consider where to start, whether to start, but the two blunt dark lines behind his forehead cause the top of his head to throb, and he cannot focus, and his mind does not give him any words to produce other than "Blessed be His name!" so he says that and feels comfort in the syllables.

As though he does not want to be distracted or misled by the prayer, the shorter blur says, "I think he was pissing his money away, flashing it around. That what you were doing, flashing money around so someone thought it was an invitation to smash your face?"

Bluett hears himself ask, "You never get any complaints from the Satin Club, is that right? I wonder what that makes you."

"What is this you say? You understand this man's Danish, Svend? He trying to say something to us?"

"Not real good," the other policeman says. "Talks like some kind of a Perker."

"I'm American!"

"Oh, he's American. Guess we better lick him up and down, then, huh?"

"Oh, fuck off," Bluett hears himself mutter. "What are you playing with me for? Leave me alone." And tries to find comfort in the monkey's words and in the odd fact that he has been visited by a monkey in a dream.

"You drunk, then, are you?" the taller blur, Svend, asks.

"Sound reasonably drunk to me," says the shorter one. The doctor leaves the room, and for some reason that frightens Bluett. No one is here to see.

"I think maybe he needs a night in the tank," the shorter one says. "Shall you have a night in the tank? Meet some of the other fellows?"

"No, please, excuse me, I'm upset," Bluett says, fear hot in his belly. He has to swallow to keep from throwing up. "I had a hard night." He winces against the sharp bitter taste rolling down his throat.

"Okay, all we ask is cooperation. You will work together with us now?"

Bluett nods, eyes squinched shut, clinging to the words of the dream monkey.

"Who fell over you?"

"Two or three men, youngish. One was blond, and very big, the one who led them. He spoke English with an accent. Maybe Polish. I went into the Satin Club for a drink. It cost three hundred kroner for a vodka, so I got out of there, and outside I got jumped by these guys. The guy who spoke was maybe Polish, maybe Russian. There were one or two others, too, but they didn't speak. Just with their feet. Maybe the others were foreign. Maybe Russian mafia." Bluett thinks if he can plant that idea in them it might lead them to the source without his having to involve the information he has on Sam, yet he cannot quite get his mind around what is happening. He wonders if they would search his house, find Sam's journals and receipts. Would the newspapers get it, would Sam's children find out?

"You have some personal knowledge of the Russian mafia?"

"Not really, no."

"'Not really' sounds like a little. You involved in something? Borrowed money? Bought some substances? Weapons? Women? If you bought something for your own personal use, you can tell us, we won't go after you."

"No," he says. "Nothing like that. Nothing."

"Then where have you heard about the Russian mafia?"

"I don't know. In the papers."

"Forget what you heard in the papers. Tell me what happened to you, what actually happened. Now, who jumped you? There on the street—not in the papers."

"I don't know. Two or three men I never saw before. Young, one of them was blond. Polish, Russian, I think."

"Would you recognize them?" The taller one does the talking now. "We can take you around in the car to see if you can spot them on the street. Sometimes they stay out, go around looking for another victim."

Bluett listens to the air in his nose. "My glasses are gone. I can't see without them. And it was dark anyway. I couldn't be sure." He considers again telling them the whole story, but no words come to his mouth. He reaches around to his pocket, checks his wallet.

"They take your money?"

"Nothing. Guess they were just out to kick someone around." He considers whether to suggest they jumped him to stop him from asking more questions in the Satin Club, considers whether that would lead to his showing the police the things Sam had in the box.

"Maybe they could not like the way you speak Danish," says the shorter policeman.

Bluett tries to focus on him, thinks *Nazi fucker*, says, "Yeah, that would be a good reason to kick me in the chest, wouldn't it? They called me a Jew now that I think of it. Called me a big-nosed Jew. The guy who broke my nose."

"Were they foreigners?"

"I already told you he was maybe Polish, maybe Russian. The others might have been Russian mafia."

"Russian criminals usally stick to their own," the taller blur says. "Were they speaking Russian? Do you speak Russian?"

"No! I—they spoke Danish. The one I heard speak."

"With accent?"

"Maybe, I don't know for sure, I had a foot in my ear."

"This gentleman is so humorous."

"Maybe he's drunk."

It occurs to Bluett that everything is worse than he imagined. Perhaps they suspect him of something because he is a victim. Victims are guilty. *Blessed be His Name!*

The foggy broad-faced doctor looks into the room again. "Don't forget, Mr. Bluett, did I tell you? See a dentist about that loose tooth in the corner of your mouth. And don't bite any apples meanwhile."

The shorter policeman sniggers. Bluett feels around inside his mouth with the tip of his tongue, finds a painful spot, pokes gingerly at it, tastes blood. The doctor steps closer. "Guess you had a rough night of it tonight, huh?"

Danish sympathy. Bluett says, "It wasn't Sunday afternoon at Tivoli." The doctor smiles appreciatively, nods with sympathy.

The taller policeman asks, "Do you have anything at all to add to your report now, Mr. Bluett? No identification possible at all? Take your time." He taps the side of his pen against his pad.

"Would you like me to write you up for crisis counseling?" the doctor asks. "Might be a good idea. Think about it."

"I don't think so."

"Think about it. Sometimes you get a delayed reaction. It helps to talk to someone."

Bluett hoists himself up to sit on the edge of the table, grunts, wincing at the sharp pull in his chest. A red-headed nurse appears with his shirt— there is dried blood down the front—and helps him slip his arms into it. "Can you do the buttons yourself?" she asks.

He nods. As his fingers work the buttons through the holes, the fuzzy tall policeman is slipping the pad back into his shirt pocket.

Bluett thinks about what has happened to him, the likely meaning of it, whether he can manage to put it together into a coherent whole and what might happen then if he does. Then he thinks about the fact that he has to get himself home. The thought of going out into the dark street again shortens his breath. He says to the policeman, "I can't see much of anything without my glasses. Could you possibly give me a ride home?"

"We could do that, *ja.*"

The nurse has his jacket and tie. She is looking closely at him, and he realizes that she is observing him, maybe for signs of dizziness, concussion. She stands close enough that he can see her face, that he can smell the soap on her skin, a slender woman with pale eyebrows.

He slides his necktie beneath his collar without tying it, and she helps him down from the table, guides his arms into the jacket and leads him to his shoes. As Bluett considers what he might say to her, she lowers herself to one knee and begins to tie his shoelace, and he says softly, "Thank you. You're very kind," hears the huskiness of his own voice.

"Wish I had one like you to come home to at night," the shorter fuzzy policeman says, and the nurse glances over her shoulder. "Scrub off," she says quietly and rises while the policemen disappear through the door.

"Think I just lost my ride," Bluett says.

She smiles, and he wishes *he* had someone like her to come home to, too. Her pale red eyebrows fascinate him. He takes a step, and his ribs pull against the tape. He groans.

"Take it still and peaceful," she says, touching his arm for moral support, as she hands him a blister pack of pills. "These are very strong. Don't take more than two every four hours. Got that?"

He nods.

"You want crutches?"

He shakes his head gingerly, sees the policemen are waiting by the outer door for him. He also sees, as the nurse hands him his Burberry, that it will have to be dry-cleaned. He hopes the blood will come out.

In the back of the police car, he watches Blegdamsvej roll past in the dark, a fuzzy blur of wall and light, and considers his options. What does he have to give them? What can he say? What can he prove? He realizes that he doesn't even know for sure himself whether the attack was a coincidence. He doesn't know anything. He doesn't know if there is the least evidence for a case against Svetlana Krylova or the Satin Club, whether some other facts could explain, or be made to explain, his own hasty conclusions. And whatever else, if he tries to go into it, he will have to reveal what was in Sam's box, just what Sam wanted to keep from being revealed.

He thinks of a poem by Dan Turèll and sniggers grimly. The poem is a parody of Dashiell Hammett's *Red Harvest* and the Turèll poem ends with someone taking a shot at the narrator, and he thinks, *Now I understood everything! Except what was happening, and why, and who was after me, and for what reason.*

It is a short ride from Rigshospitalet to his apartment on the lakes. The taller policeman gets out and opens the door for him, supports his elbow as he swings his legs out slowly, one at a time, and hoists him to his feet. Bluett grimaces.

"Want help up the stairs?" the policeman asks.

"No. Thanks for your help."

"Okay, you think of anything else, just call the station."

"Who should I ask for?"

"Whoever answers will help you. They'll have our report. We'll be out now looking for a group of troublemakers. They might still be roaming around drunk. If we find anyone you'll be contacted for a confrontation."

Is that a threat? he wonders. *A warning?* And he realizes that he is half-way worrying that the police are part of a conspiracy, recognizes that for what it is and decides all he needs now is sleep.

"Give you some good advices," the taller policeman says in English in a not unfriendly manner. "Stay away from those Satin Club places. Find yourself a nice woman your own age. Man your age shouldn't be running after young whores in places like that. Only bring you to troubles."

Bluett grunts, smacks the car door shut after him.

He lets himself in and climbs the winding wooden stairs slowly, gets the key into the lock on his door after a few tries, hits the switch for the overhead light and goes immediately for the dresser drawer where he thinks he can remember having stored his old glasses just in case. He finds them in the bottom drawer in a plastic case, an old pair of tortoise-framed plastic lenses. The one earpiece is stained with white streaks of discoloration, and they fit loosely, but his heart floods with gratitude at the ingenuity of opticians as the world around him adjusts into focus.

All the necessary things available in a society, the pool of ingenuity. Eyeglasses, medical care, food, housing . . . That's what holds us together. Commerce. He pictures living in the woods, in a tree. Never could. Trapped in civilization. Instead of bears in the forest you got the Russian mafia. And police protection instead of a spear. Only hope is to keep clear of it all. Don't go into the forest at night.

Then he remembers the dream monkey, suddenly wonders at the vividness of the image of the prayer, like a shrill psalm: *Blessed be His name!*

He hobbles out to his oak table, lowers himself into a chair, considering his next move. He glances at his wristwatch: The crystal is shattered, the digital display blank. The clock on his stereo says 3:56. Nothing to do now but try to sleep. His ribs and nose are throbbing, first in unison, then in counterpoint, and he begins to notice a number of other sore and tender points on his back, his right, his rump. His right hand hurts and he notices the heel of his left is scraped badly. He feels less anger than bafflement. How odd that such things transpire.

Then, glancing through the open door into the little hall, he spots something white that had apparently been slipped under the door on the carpet, an envelope. He hoists himself to his feet and limps over to it, squats slowly, catches it between thumb and forefinger, rises, muttering, and proceeds to the kitchen, where he fills a glass of water from the tap and pops two of the pills from the blister pack the nurse gave him.

It occurs to him she did not tell him what they were, whether there were side effects, whether it is dangerous to mix them with alcohol; but they would always claim that anyway. She only said they were very strong. Morphine maybe. Ketogan. Would they make him sleepy?

Standing over the kitchen counter, he looks at the envelope. It trembles in his fingers. It is plain, cheap gray paper, nothing written on it. He peels back the self-adhesive flap. There are photos inside. He holds them in the circle of light from the ceiling lamp.

The first shows Sam wearing stockings and a garter belt and bra. He stands facing three seated persons viewed from the back. Sam is the only identifiable person in the picture. His hands are behind him like a soldier at parade rest, and he looks very happy. To one side of him is a person wearing a leather mask and wielding a paddle.

In the next, he is on a table with his ankles tied into gynecological stirrups while a woman, again viewed from behind, holds a black dildo above him. He is smiling like a puppy dog.

The last shows him tied naked to a cross. A woman, viewed from behind, stands in front of him holding a whip alongside her leg. Sam is not smiling. The quality of the photo and composition are poor, making it seem even more seedy.

Bluett tucks the photos back into the envelope. He limps back to the oak table, switching off the lamp on the way, and sits staring out into the dark morning. He finds he is most comfortable sitting straight up, his back even with the back of the chair. He nods there, thinking perhaps the pills are also a soporific, but wakes again a few moments later. It occurs to him that Sam died, that Sam paid out the equivalent of a couple of million crowns to keep these photos from being shown to his ex-wife and children. He can imagine no other explanation for this. Simple. Svetlana Krylova won his trust, extracted information, determined his weak spot, applied the pressure. He paid her, then killed himself both to stop the extortion and in shame for having been caught in a trap fashioned for him of his own hunger.

Still there is the question why, when he knew he was going to kill himself, he hadn't burned the stuff in the box. Bluett dozes again, wakes, noting that his broken bones have stopped throbbing except in the most distant, almost beneficent manner, his bruises numbed. He realizes he ought to try to sleep while the pain is gone, supports himself on the edge of the table as he straightens his knees, notices again the envelope on the oak table, thinks. Maybe he just wanted to feel that one other person in the world, one friend, might know him, might understand him, might know him and not hate him for what he knew.

You took it all too seriously, Sam. Yet how would I have felt in your place, thinking of those pictures being shown to your kids? Maybe she just asked for it a little bit at a time and you kept thinking you could just give her that much and that much more until you were so deep in, it was all too late.

Undressing is an ordeal, but finally his clothes lie in a pool on the bedroom floor, and he sidles in under the feather blanket. Ugly thoughts come to him as he lies there. An article he read in the *New Yorker* recently about a cult in Nebraska where the leader decreed that wayward members could be declared slaves, that torture was an acceptable means of correction with murder as the extreme necessity. The leader's name was Ryan and the article included excerpts from the court transcript of some of the things Ryan had done to his followers and to their children, how he had taped the mouth of one to muffle his screams, and, using razor blade and pliers, had literally skinned him alive. Bluett could not believe what he was reading, yet it was quoted directly from a court record, as reported in the *New Yorker* magazine.

Bluett feels feverish there beneath the blanket, feels as though his brain has shaken loose, and he is spinning. His thoughts sink slowly away from him and his brain calms into sleep, but not before he sees again, for a fleeting instant, the monkey: *Blessed be His name!*

At some point he rises again to consciousness and opens his eyes to see the snout of a black dog against a blood-red sky staring into his face. He is not frightened. He thinks simply that this must be death, come to take him, and closes his eyes again and sinks into a place of fragments where existence drifts on the water of consciousness through a long channel of blankness that eddies into a patch of images: a street of many people where he walks again in the dusk to some unknown place. There are too many dreams to remember, too strange and wordless, one that is the broken fragment of a rib, a curved jagged bone, an object that knows pain without mercy. He steps off the subway onto a high, narrow, stilted bridge and requests information at the booth but cannot understand the language spoken by the black woman there. The bridge sways on its stilts high above the road. He clutches the railing and then his mother is there, very thin and naked, her nipples, and he offers her his comforter, and is grateful then to breach the surface of sleep and understand he is awake in his own dark bedroom, his nose clogged with dried blood, mouth arid.

He eases out of bed and hobbles to the kitchen for water that he gulps from the tap. He clears his nose, tries to fathom what day it is, remembers what has happened to him. He thinks he needs help to come through this and finds himself at the door, about to go to Sam, but remembers his friend's eyes staring at him wordlessly, imprinted in him.

In the bedroom, he looks at his watch, which is cracked and blank, sighs, phones the time operator, learns that it is 2:13 A.M. on Tuesday. Two days have passed. He ought to eat.

On the kitchen counter are two blackened bananas. He gobbles them with a glass of skimmed milk, refills the milk tumbler, stands smacking his lips at the kitchen window, looking across to the dark wall, the dark line of rooftops, a shaved white globe of moon peering down through the window with dusty pale light. The sheepdog is lying outside the door in the courtyard, chin on paws. For some reason he makes Bluett think of the monkey in his dream, but the monkey is no longer vivid. He doesn't hear the words of its psalm, and the dog does not look up at him.

He finds the blister pack of pills and eats two of them, crawls back into bed.

The sound his telephone makes is hateful to him as it burbles into the peace of his sleep. His eyes open. The ringing has stopped. Or did he only dream it? He sits up and pain rises through his chest to his nose. The pain is familiar now, no longer so worrying, only a dim reminder of the fragility of his bones.

He sits up on the edge of the bed, sees daylight at the window, but his eyes are too heavy to care to look out. Then the telephone is burbling again.

His voice sounds different in his own ears, resonating through the cracked bone as he speaks into the receiver. "Yeah?"

"Mr. Bluett?"

"Yeah?"

"This is Anders Finglas."

Bluett lifts to the sound, sits up straight in the chair by the phone. "Hello, Anders, how are you? How are you doing?"

"I thought you might like to know about the funeral services. Dad will be cremated at Garnison's this Friday."

"Friday? Excuse me. I've been ill. What day is it?"

"It's Tuesday. There are still some formalities at the Forensics Institute, but we have been able to set the ceremony for Friday. Ten A.M."

"Forensics?"

"Yeah, they always do that with a . . . when someone takes his life."

Jesus. "Anders, thank you so much for telling me. I'll be there. Friday. At ten."

"There was a strange thing," the boy says. "They didn't find any cancer. They didn't find anything at all."

"Nothing at all?"

"No, nothing. No cancer, no sickness."

Bluett's mind is lifting through the heaviness, returning to a place he has already abandoned.

"It must have been something else."

"Maybe," Bluett says, "maybe he was just depressed, very . . . depressed, and *thought* he was ill . . ."

"You mentioned that he was together with someone, a woman. I heard you say that to the policeman."

"I, uh, I spoke too rashly there, Anders. I didn't really know anything. I don't really. Sam mentioned something in passing once, but I didn't really know anything at all about it. I spoke without thinking. Off the top of my head. But I do know he was depressed. I could see it, last time we were together. If only I could have done something, but it was . . . he just didn't want to talk."

That done, there is still the box, the pictures. But he cannot think now for the pain across his nose. On the bathroom shelf is the blister pack, two pills remaining. He throws them into his mouth and takes water from the tap into the cup of his hand to wash them down, and his eyes are already closing as he makes his way back to the bed.

He does not know how much time has passed, but when he wakes again, he thinks perhaps he is beginning to feel better. He realizes he must call the unemployment insurance office to apply for compensation for these days of missed production, looks at the clock on the stereo, but it is the middle of the night. He puts his head back to the pillow, expecting to sink, but his eyes are open, his mind clear.

Get up. Eat. He shuffles to the kitchen, pops open the refrigerator. Three eggs, butter, tomato juice. The juice brings the memory of Sam's eyes again. He scrambles the eggs, makes toast, eats from the frying pan standing at the kitchen counter and when he has forked the last of the egg into his mouth, he spoons marmalade on the last half-piece of toast, drains his glass of tomato juice, pours more, drinks again.

Palms on the counter edge, he licks his teeth and thinks he might be well now. He thinks of music, but somehow he does not want music just now. He wants silence, stillness. His ribs ache only a little as his hand reaches up for the Stoli bottle. He fills a tumbler with ice and sits on his sofa, pours.

The ice cracks and steams beneath the clear liquor, and he lifts the glass.

He finds himself staring across the room at the mask with the cork-screw eyes. The smell of the vodka seeps into his cut nose, and he does not think he can drink. The eyes have fixed on him. The mask is full of mock-ery and his stomach turns with the smell of the liquor. The eyes seem to spiral, drawing him, even as he recognizes the thought as nonsense, and it occurs to him those insane corkscrew eyes have monitored his life, have seen everything, mute, blank, staring witness of it all, mocking him, and it might have been himself hung there on the wall, a dead wooden face that saw everything and did not speak and did nothing.

His hand is tight on the glass, trembling, and it too, the glass, the clear cold liquor, mocks him, a glass of mockery with a vile stench. His breath heaves in his lungs, his heart bangs behind the sore broken ribcage, and all at once, he sees beyond a blankness in his mind a pair of eyes. Sam's eyes, staring mutely from the other side while he sat and watched his friend, thinking, *What? What is it, Sam? Tell me. I can't see into your mind. I can't see what you're thinking. Tell me!*

Why hadn't he spoken? Why hadn't he insisted, demanded. *Sam, what's wrong? Tell me what it is, Sam. What can I do for you, buddy? What? Don't go, I won't let you, stay here and talk it out with me!*

He is on his feet and his hand lifts back as he hears the cry escape his throat and the glass flies, spraying vodka back across his own face. The tumbler smashes on the wall, but it is not enough, he has the bottle by the neck.

You fucking no-good stinking loathesome fucking . . .

For a splintered moment he sees what he will do, and then he is only the doing of it as the bottle shatters across the corkscrew eyes.

Glass fragments geyser outward on the stinking liquor. The mask plunges to the floor, and he is on his knees over its dull wood obverse, a jagged crack stitched open.

He has never before heard such sounds as issue from his throat. He might have been a woman, a child, the shameless tortured sounds that left him as Sam's eyes watched him there, finally knowing one another, finally seeing one another and neither able to speak, to ask, to offer a single word.

And Bluett thinks, *A woman would have asked, would have insisted to know, a woman would not have succumbed to Sam's silence . . .*

He sleeps again, rises in the dark once more and hobbles to the living room, smells the repulsive stench of vodka. Stepping carefully over the shards of glass, he opens windows, gets the vacuum cleaner from the cupboard. He wraps the cracked mask in newspaper and lays it on a closet shelf. Then he vacuums up the glass.

When the rug is clean and the freezing night air has chased the stench of liquor, he closes the windows, drinks a glass of water from the tap, returns to bed and closes his eyes, sleeps.

Then there is a sound reaching in to him. The telephone. He opens his eyes—it is day—throws back the covers, moving too quickly, sits groaning on the edge of the bed as pain shoots out from his ribs, and the phone keeps ringing. He speaks to it as he hobbles across the living room carpet, "All right, all right, all right, I'm coming, keep your pants on."

It stops before he gets to it. He turns, smacking his tongue, thinks of juice. The phone rings again before he can look at the clock. He speaks into the receiver and listens tensely, his heart lifting to hear Raffaella's voice.

"El," he says. "Hi, honey, how are you?"

"Fine, thank you."

"Well, that's good. What's happening?" Staring out the window, he can see the lake has begun to melt. The surface is soupy, and patches of broken ice reveal water rippling in the breeze. "What time is it now, anyway?" he asks, playing with his upper canine with the tip of his tongue. It is wobbly and he tastes blood.

"Around three thirty."

"God, I slept half the week away, more. You want to join me for lunch or something, El? Dinner?" He remembers his face then. "But don't get shocked when you see me. I've got a bandage on my nose and a few bruises. Hey, you can bring Jens-Martin if you want."

"Oh, Dad," she says. "It's all *shit*."

"You two have a fight?"

"He is *so* . . ." When she does not speak further, he asks, "Is it serious?"

"Who knows? Who *cares*?"

"You want to come stay over here for a while?"

"Could I?"

"You bet you could. Listen, you got any money? Pick up a couple good steaks on the way, I'll pay you back. I'm hungry. We'll have us a nice dinner here. I've got some wine. I'll pay you for the steaks."

He hangs up and stands at the window watching sunlight ripple on the cold melted water, the edges of broken ice, his tongue playing at his tooth. On the other side, two swans swim in the melted water. He goes to the bathroom mirror to look at his loose tooth, but he can see nothing other than that he looks like hell. The swelling of his mouth has gone down, but there is still a red bruise across the side of his face. His forehead, too, is bruised, and the white tape across his nose is dirty.

You were lucky, he thinks, looking at himself. *You can still walk. Your head is intact.*

Gently he sponges his face with a hot washcloth, washes beneath his arms, his groin. He washes his hands thoroughly, runs water over his scraped palm, scrubs and trims his fingernails, cleans his teeth, careful to avoid the loose canine. As best he can, he sponges dirt from the bandage on his nose so it appears more presentable.

He wonders if he will ever feel safe on the street again, thinks about acquiring a weapon, but cannot imagine himself using it. He certainly could not use a knife or a sap. Perhaps he could wield a pistol, but then he might use it, and the thought of firing bullets into someone is abhorrent. He would end in jail himself and the thought of that is worse than abhorrent. Defenseless. But you need some kind of defense, protection.

Those men were sent, he realizes with certainty. They were definitely sent. Just like the photographs. It was a message, a warning. Persist and we break your back. We send the pictures to Sam's kids and ex-wife. The very thing he killed himself to avoid, so his death will have been utterly pointless. Their power to blackmail is dead with Sam. Except for this pressure to keep Bluett's mouth shut out of respect for his friend's memory. For that matter, out of fear of another beating. *I'm no fucking hero.*

What would it do for Sam's son to know the details?

Nothing.

So they win?

Yeah. They win. What they got out of it. Let them choke on it. Let them have their own filthy world to themselves.

Then there is a knock on the door, and Raffaella is there, clucking over her father's bruised face. He enjoys the attention for a bit, then tells her it looks a lot worse than it is, tells her it was some drunk on Nyhavn, nothing important, no serious damage.

"Want a drink, honey?"

"Got any Coke?"

He takes Coke, too, and they chat, about the melting lake, the end of winter, the lengthening days—here it is, nearly five, and still half light. El tells him something his son said about him recently, about how cozy he is as a father, and Bluett feels the water in his eyes. "Timothy said that?"

She nods several times, smiling, happy to see how happy it makes him. She does not mention Jens-Martin again, and he doesn't ask, allowing her to take her time coming around to it. She puts on a Carole King CD. She says she is studying that CD for her singing lessons. Then she takes the CD off and sings a number for him a cappella that she is working on. "Will You Still Love Me Tomorrow?" She sings it slow, strong-voiced, contemplatively, and Bluett closes his eyes in gratitude that he did not skimp on the lessons, that she would care to sing the song for him.

"You sing like an angel," he says when she is finished.

"Oh quit exaggeratin', Dad," she tells him, her cheeks flushed with pleasure.

In the kitchen they work together to prepare the steaks, two beautiful slabs of entrecôte she bought from the ecological butcher on Frederiksborggade. She washes lettuce, quarters tomatoes, dices cucumber, while he peels an onion before the open window, cold water running, mixes a dressing of olive oil and seven-year-old Balsamico red wine vinegar, mustard, sea salt and freshly ground pepper. She has also bought a little plastic tub of fresh béarnaise, which he heats slowly in a saucepan. He shoves a platter of frozen oven-ready fries beneath the grill, pops a frozen baguette into the oven, and spills half an envelope of frozen peas into boiling water.

With a clean linen cloth spread across the oak table, he uncorks a bottle of Pomerol and puts on Mozart's Horn Concertos and lights a candle in the old-fashioned brass stick his ex-wife gave him for Christmas once.

They get lucky with the steaks, perfect medium-rare and tender, and she doesn't talk about Jens-Martin at all.

"The birds are back on the lake," he says.

She nods. "Maybe we should take a walk down and feed them some bread afterward."

"Let's do that," he says.

She runs a French fry through the béarnaise on her plate, munches, smiling. "Dad, 'member when you used to sing to me at bedtime?"

"You bet I do."

"You used to sing 'Mr. Blue' and 'I had a dog and his name was Blue' and 'Eileen Og.'"

"You remember all that?"

"I loved it," she says and starts to cry. He comes around the table and lays an arm around her shoulder, squeezes, and his heart is flooded with gratitude that she has come to him for comfort as he says, "Hey, honey, it's okay, it's all okay, your dad is here for you."

She wipes away the tears with the heels of her hands, and Bluett returns to his side of the table, refills their wine glasses.

He thinks a moment and tells her about the monkey he dreamed, how vivid it was, tall and scrawny, and how it said in a piping voice, *Blessed be His name!* Though the memory is no longer vivid—only a memory of its vividness.

There is wonder in her gray eyes as she listens to her father. "That's amazing," she whispers. "Where did it come from?"

He shrugs, shakes his head in bewilderment, but is comforted by her amazement, her enthusiasm at the image.

"It's like, what do they call it? Like an *archetype*, you know, Dad?"

The phone rings. Bluett goes to it, trying to minimize his limp, puts it to his ear and listens tensely. "'Lo."

Jens-Martin. He apologizes for the interruption, asks for Raffaella. Bluett pretends not to listen as she speaks on the phone but cannot miss the sound of her voice changing from chill to forgiving, hears her accept an apology, twice. "It's okay. I understand. It's okay. I know you were under pressure."

She replaces the receiver and her step is light returning to the table.

"Everything okay again?"

She nods brightly. "I guess I won't stay the night after all, if you don't mind."

"Just remember, honey," he says, "you always have a place here, you always have a home here as long as you need it. It's not big but we could fix it up so we each had our own space if ever you needed a place to turn to."

They have coffee and After Eights, and he gives her a bag of old bread to throw to the birds on her way back.

He stands at the window and watches as she walks her bicycle across to the embankment, sees the phosphorescent shapes of swans gliding toward her in the dark as she brakes and pitches clumps of bread out into the water. Then she is shaking the last of the crumbs from the plastic bag, which she stuffs into the pocket of her red quilted jacket. She swings her leg onto the bike, glances up at his window. He realizes she knew he was watching. It makes him happy that she knew, that she knows him. She waves, and peddles off along the embankment to the bridge.

Bluett clears the table, rinses the dishes and stacks them, decides to let them be. He pours himself a Hennessy, flicks off the kitchen light.

Then he thinks of something.

From the top of his closet he takes down the "dossier" envelope from the box Sam had stored with him. He stuffs it into the garbage bag beneath his kitchen sink. The garbage collectors come on Thursday. He will put the bag down into the dumpster early tomorrow morning, and wait and watch as they take it away to be burned. And that will be the end of it.

Out of his desk drawer, he gets the envelope with the photos of Sam in it. Without opening it again, he lights the edge of it on the flame of the candle on the dining table, holds it down to let the flame climb, and drops it in the big metal ashtray. He watches the blue tongues of flame lick around it and grow, his nose pulling against the stench of burnt photo paper lifting to his nostrils, and he thinks, *Ah Sam, it was just silliness, that's the tragedy. You let it get away with you and then you got caught, but it was all just silliness, you poor guy. If only . . .*

He wonders what he himself would have done in a similar situation, to protect his own children from disillusionment.

It was just bad luck, Sam. Bad judgment and bad luck. If only I had not let you go back to your apartment. If only I had insisted that we talk it through.

The last bit of blue-yellow flame curls out, leaving ash and paper stub.

Let them choke on it, he thinks. *Let them live choking*. And wonders how he will ever be able to find peace and forgiveness for himself, if he will have to carry Sam's staring eyes with him for the rest of his life.

The stereo is silent now. He clicks it open and slides in Coltrane's *A Love Supreme*. He turns his armchair to face the window and inhales the bouquet of the Hennessy, sips, thinking of the years it took to produce this taste, the planning, the confidence that you would still be there, someone would still be there twenty, thirty years later to tap the kegs.

That's what I like about Europe, he thinks, as Coltrane blows the opening formal bars of "Acknowledgement" and introduces the theme.

Idly Bluett reaches to the windowsill for the jagged cool-white crystal there, takes it in his palm, wonders half-seriously if it would signal her.

Then he puts it back on the sill, and reaches for the phone.

Her voice is bright at the sound of his.

"I was wondering," he says. "A good friend of mine, his funeral is being held on Friday. I was wondering if you would come with me."

There is a silence.

"It would mean a lot to me," he says.

"Yes," she whispers. "Of course. I am glad that you would ask me. How are you?"

"I'm okay. I've missed you."

"I have missed you, too. Wery much. All these thoughts have been turning through my mind," she says. "I think of you and I think of my ex-husbands, how it never worked with them, how it all went wrong, and wondering why I wanted so much for it to be the same with you."

He realizes how much he wants to see her, to have her here with him, to touch her. No questions, just two people, two friends, lovers, the best of friends.

"Would you like to come over?" he asks. "I would like so much to see you."

"Give me half an hour," she says.

He places the phone back in the cradle, puts aside his cognac snifter, and waits for her. Down along the bank, a jogger bobs past in the shadow of the streetlamp, and Coltrane's tenor loosens the fist of his mind so it can move with the urgency of the notes to escape form, to find the source of cohesion, vibration. The music moves like a current inside him, like a phosphorescent angel that defies form, that fills his chest, his mind, his heart. Up above, Hale-Bopp glows in the dark vault of the sky, and across the embankment, the red neon egg shimmers, vanishing into the black melting lake.

A NOTE ON THE AUTHOR

Born and raised in New York, Thomas E. Kennedy has lived and worked in Copenhagen for three decades. His books include novels, story and essay collections, literary criticism, translation, and anthologies. *Beneath the Neon Egg* is the final novel of his acclaimed Copenhagen Quartet to be published in the United States, following *In the Company of Angels* (2010), *Falling Sideways* (2011), and *Kerrigan in Copenhagen* (2013). He teaches in the M.F.A. in creative writing program at Fairleigh Dickinson University. Kennedy recorded his translations of works of the late beatnik Danish poet Dan Turèll set to music by the renowned international composer Halfdan E, released on CD by PlantSounds records in 2013. Kennedy's websites are www.CopenhagenQuartet.com and www.thomasekennedy.com.